REANIMATED REX

ALSO BY ALEX EBENSTEIN

Melon Head Mayhem
Curse Corvus

REANIMATED REX

ALEX EBENSTEIN

REANIMATED REX

REANIMATED REX

Content warnings are available at the end of this book. Please consult this list for any particular subject matter you may be sensitive to.

For the dino kids who never gave it up.

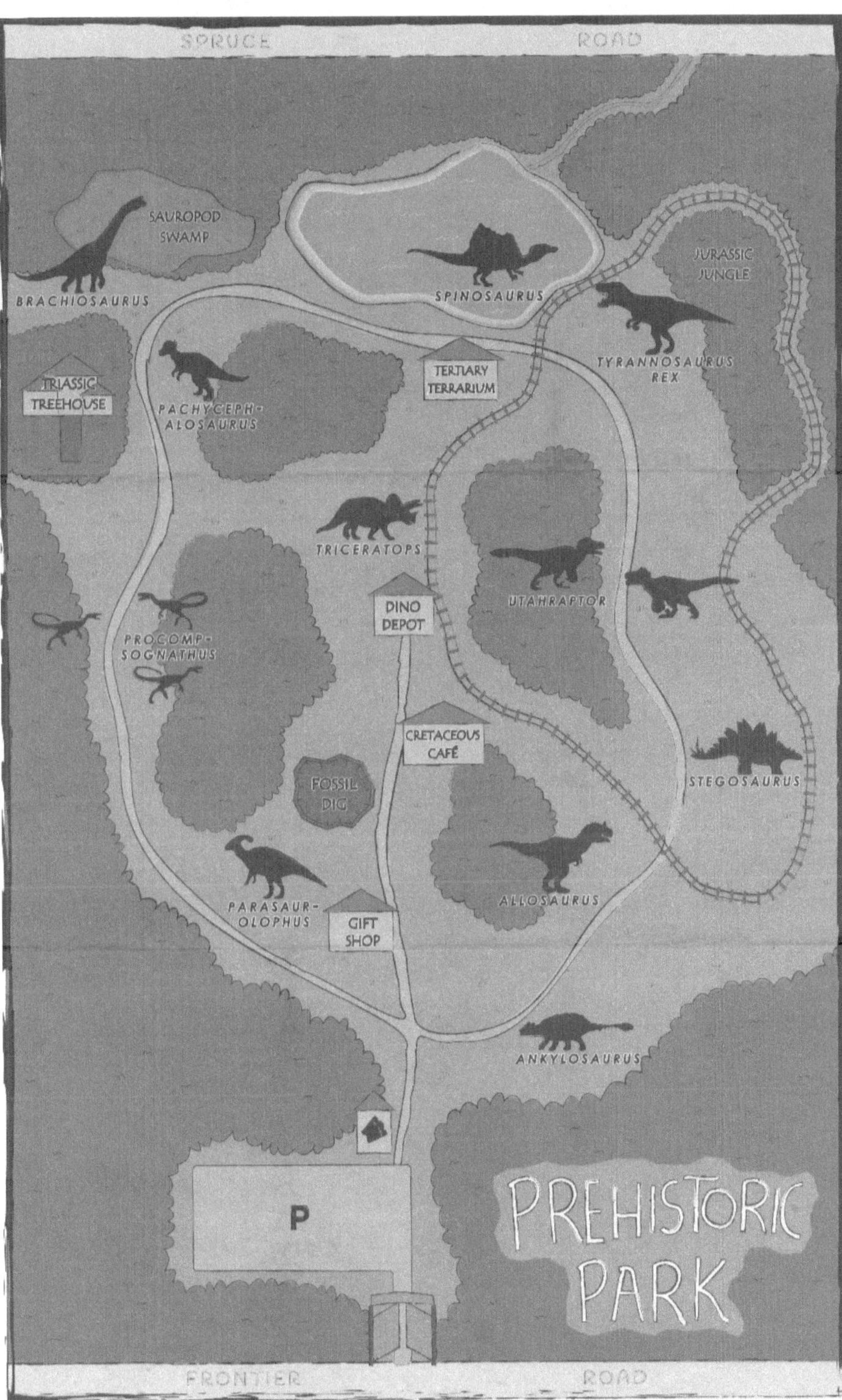

SPRUCE
ROAD
SAUROPOD SWAMP
BRACHIOSAURUS
SPINOSAURUS
JURASSIC JUNGLE
TYRANNOSAURUS REX
TRIASSIC TREEHOUSE
PACHYCEPH- ALOSAURUS
TERTIARY TERRARIUM
TRICERATOPS
UTAHRAPTOR
PROCOMP- SOGNATHUS
DINO DEPOT
CRETACEOUS CAFÉ
STEGOSAURUS
FOSSIL DIG
ALLOSAURUS
PARASAUR- OLOPHUS
GIFT SHOP
ANKYLOSAURUS
P
PREHISTORIC PARK
FRONTIER
ROAD

PROLOGUE

They pushed him out of the car without ever coming to a stop.

Joel wasn't mad about it—he never expected to survive the night completely unscathed—though he did land hard on the gravel shoulder of the road, and a jagged stone ripped a hole in the right knee of his chinos. It wasn't called hazing because of all the joy and laughter, at least not for the target.

The curious thing he couldn't determine, as he brushed the dirt from his pants and turned his phone flashlight on, was whether their moving drop-off and speedy retreat were due to strong play-acting, or from genuine fear of this place.

The first low rumble of approaching thunder reminded Joel he was on the clock. Damian told him he'd circle around the long country roads and pass the front entrance every five minutes. But the third time would be the last. If Joel wasn't back with his souvenir within fifteen minutes, he'd have to walk home. Not a prospect he cherished with a five-mile walk and a storm due any minute. He had to get in, get out.

The light from his phone could only illuminate about ten feet in front of him, but it would have to be enough. At the edge of his field of light stood the fifteen-foot, wooden slat privacy fence. Joel walked on the shoulder, guiding his beam along until the entrance to the park appeared. Even in direct light, the driveway looked like little more than an old two-track, so quickly had the road-side vegetation taken back over. The main gate, however, was hard to miss.

Two pillars bigger around than Joel could reach flanked either side. Between, there were more of the wooden slats like the surrounding fence, only constructed into two swinging doors. At least, he assumed they'd once swung. Now they were secured together by several cross-laying boards nailed down. Above, a wide plank hung broken in two, splitting the words painted in faux-archaic letters.

Nodding, Joel recalled the instructions given by Brian as they rode out to the middle of bumfuck nowhere where the derelict theme park moldered.

Ten paces to the left of the main gate there are two slats rotted away at the ground. That's where you'll get in.

The knee-high grass rustled against his legs as he tramped to the left gate pillar. Holding the phone in his left hand with the light pointed to the ground and trailing his right hand along the rough fence, he paced off the requisite ten steps. As promised, two slats were missing chunks near the ground, though the tall grass would have hidden it well from passers-by. The hole was not large, however, and for once in his young life, Joel was thankful to have a narrow frame. Wanting both hands free to pull himself through, if need be, he pocketed his phone and kneeled.

Pausing, he took a final deep breath before shoving his head through the gap in the fence. Damian and the others had told him all the rumors. The dark, overgrown wilds of an abandoned land. A psychopathic recluse residing somewhere on the property. And, of course, the strange noises on stormy nights—the very reason this "initiation" had to happen now. Joel couldn't tell for sure if any of them truly believed the legend, but he, brand new to the area, thought the whole thing smelled of bullshit. That said, he'd have done anything to make a good impression on the crew, knowing otherwise his Junior year as the 'new kid' at Buckman High would be a nightmare.

Find the gift shop located somewhere in the middle of the park and grab a dinosaur figurine—that was the objective. And time was ticking.

Time to go.

His leading hand did little to flatten the tall grass beyond the gate, so the dewy blades assaulted his face on the way through. Some poked, others clawed, and still others tried sticking to his smooth skin and tangled hair. His nostrils met the musky scent of petrichor, not entirely unpleasant, as he dug into the ground and pulled while simultaneously pushing off with his feet on the other side. Soon, he was inside the park.

After jumping up, his first move was to grab his phone and relight the flashlight. Thanks to years of neglect—and to the darkness—there was not much to be seen other than the expected overgrowth of plants. The driveway, however, was still somewhat visible, so he followed that at a jog.

He had no plan or map, only the knowledge that the gift shop was in the middle somewhere, though he figured it had to be along the main drive and path in because that was also the way out. And what better place to snag tourists for a last-minute purchase?

The driveway came to an abrupt end. Joel hazarded a quick scan to his left. He couldn't see much or very far, but it looked to be an expansive area that was likely once the parking lot. Moving on, he followed the remnants of the old lot to where it narrowed to a walking path.

Immediately to the left was a ticket booth, partially lit up by a distant blip of lightning. Thunder quickly followed—a second, at most, which meant the storm was about to arrive. He didn't linger. Onward.

The first dinosaur he saw made him scream.

He knew they were there—it was Prehistoric Park after all—but the hulking thing surprised him, materializing into view of his cone of light. Joel didn't know which dinosaur because he wasn't a nerd, but it was enormous and long-necked like a reptilian giraffe. At any rate, he was thankful Damian and the crew were nowhere near when he freaked, because even after returning with a prize he might not have recovered from the embarrassment.

Continuing along the path he saw myriad signs, but they were impossible to decipher under years of detritus and decay. As he jogged, he lit up his phone screen to check the clock. It'd been seven minutes since crash-landing in front of the entrance. The crew would have driven past once already. He couldn't afford to waste a single minute now.

As luck would have it, the main building soon came into view. In the same archaic-looking letters as the park entrance, the words GIFT SHOP appeared above the door. There was no actual door anymore, however, a curious thing that Joel didn't have time to speculate on.

Two dinosaurs guarded either side of the empty frame, though not well. Perhaps at one time they did, but now one had fallen, or been tipped over, blocking the lower half of the entrance. They were the same type—about his height but much longer, with a long snout of snarling teeth—which felt vaguely familiar to Joel, though he couldn't remember ever seeing a feathery dinosaur like that in movies. Weren't all those dinosaurs supposed to be big reptiles, hard and scaly? At any rate, these ones *were* hard; life-sized models made from something like fiberglass or maybe sculpted. What Joel needed was a miniature version, hopefully found just inside the building.

Carefully, he stepped over the replica and slunk inside. As if waiting for him to do so, the first drops of rain arrived, pattering against the terracotta roof tiles.

His phone flashlight did better in the enclosed room. Not that he needed extra help. The shelves in the gift shop looked to be as fully-stocked as when the place was operational. There were souvenirs everywhere. Closest to him were t-shirts and hoodies with "Prehistoric Park" screen-printed across their fronts. If he didn't think he'd get in trouble someday being spotted in one, he would have snagged a shirt. At any rate, they were not his target.

What he wanted was on the back wall, lining dusty shelves.

Picking his way through the ruins and layers of roaming vegetation, Joel found his way to the back of the shop and selected a dinosaur. There was only one of its kind left. He grabbed the small dino and, as he did so, noticed a label underneath that he could just make out.

"*Utahraptor*," he whispered. "Hmm."

The room filled with white light and a massive *CRACK!* resounded, startling Joel into dropping the figurine.

"Shit." He bent quickly to gather it up again and found himself near another doorway he'd missed before. There was a larger door and hallway across the room that he assumed led to an exhibit, but this one before him appeared to be for a staff or mechanical closet.

He would have ignored it—should have—but right then he noticed a red-tinged light coming from within.

Has the power not been shut off? he wondered, and despite himself and the ticking clock, shuffled towards it.

The red light came from a board with buttons and switches. Everything else was dark except for this one spot, where the words "EMERGENCY ON/OFF" were lit in red above a large switch, currently sitting at "OFF".

"Could it be?" he whispered, though he could barely hear his own words over the din of rain and growing wind. Between his eyes having adjusted to the darkness and the red light, Joel could see well enough to pocket his phone. Grasping the switch, he had a wild thought: *How cool would I be if I turned power back on to the park? Lit the sonofabitch up? I would be a legend at school!*

It was naive, stupid thinking, but it was enough.

Joel threw the switch to "ON" and took a step back.

Nothing happened for a couple seconds, just long enough for him to groan in disappointment. But soon a whirring came from somewhere within the mechanical equipment, the tell-tale sound of things warming and winding up.

A dim bulb above his head came on.

He grinned. "Hell ye—"

A simultaneous flash and crack struck, the air so suddenly heavy and loud Joel could feel the pressure. The boom shook the building.

And worse: the board crackled, popped, and sparks began to fly.

"Shit, shit, shit." He reached for the switch, but halfway to it the light went out and the whirring abruptly stopped. Nothing but storm noises again.

Leave it alone. You have what you came for, now go.

And he did. After retrieving his phone, Joel wheeled around and rushed through the gift shop ruins. He paused briefly at the door to mentally prepare himself, then ran through the empty door frame out into the driving rain.

The downpour reduced visibility significantly, but Joel always had a pretty good sense of direction which he relied on now to head back the way he'd come. It was nearly a straight shot anyway, so he wasn't worried. The occasional lightning flash helped, too. Although, in the back of his mind, he worried he'd run into a bout of piss poor luck and get struck by lightning right as he reached the fence. That would figure.

A low sound like a growl from somewhere behind him tugged at his attention as he ran. He couldn't help his first thoughts from screaming, *DINOSAUR!*—but that was silly…right? He couldn't afford the time to investigate that thought process further, though, so his bothered brain coped by inserting flits of images and past experiences of storm noises as a source. They satisfied the worry, at least temporarily, anyway.

The clock told him he had a minute left, suggesting he hurry.

Joel pumped his arms as the rain intensified, pelting his exposed skin. His clothes were soaked through and clinging to his body. The phone flashlight bounced erratically, making the path nearly impossible to see, but he had to continue to trust his feet and his natural sense of direction. An odd-sounding boom of thunder struck, reverberating more like a bellow, though he couldn't remember seeing a flash of lightning close enough to warrant the noise.

Since when did thunder bellow?

Stop it, stop it, stop it! You've freaked yourself out. Just run, damnit, run!

He felt a slight change in footing before he saw the path had become the driveway. A giggle of giddy excitement puffed out with his huffing breath. He was so close now. He was going to make it.

A flash and immediate crack clattered the world around him, causing Joel to flinch and yelp. He nearly fell, too, but at the last second caught his footing and stayed upright. The lightning, however, illuminated the air enough for him to see the fence and exactly where he needed to go. He could close the distance and hit his target with his eyes shut, he thought, except—

Except, something was off in the afterimage burned into his eyeballs. The fence was there, exactly where it should have been. But the fence didn't look like it should have. He hadn't bothered to look behind him after coming through the hole on his way in, but he knew what a wooden slat privacy fence looked like front and back: more or less the same, aside from the supports on the inside. This fence didn't look like that. Not in the brief glance Joel got from the lightning.

On cue, another bolt lit up the scene, confirming what he saw the first time.

This fence was *fortified*. Steel beams, a metal lattice covering between each of them, and looping spools of razor wire.

Man, this can't be right, Joel thought. *All this, to keep people out of an abandoned theme park? Unless, someone's trying to keep something…in?*

He continued to run toward it, though, because what choice did he have?

Mercifully, he found the hole in the fence right away. He lingered for a second, wanting to examine the fortification, wanting to touch it, understand it. But no, he shoved his phone—*uh oh, time's up*—into his pocket and dove to the ground. With the hand still grasping the dino figurine leading the way, he shoved forward.

Joel saw Damian's Jeep just down the road, forty feet away, Damian and Julie faintly lit by the dash lights.

The dinosaur in his hand caught his eye again, and with it came a much-too-late realization: the knocked over dinosaur statue had not been blocking the door on his way out of the gift shop.

A blinding bolt of lightning split the sky.

"Oh, shit."

He felt the piercing sensations first, covering multiple spots along his left calf. The vice-like pressure came immediately after. Joel tried to scream but lost most of it as something yanked him back inside the park.

Joel jerked his leg, trying to free it from whatever gripped him, but a stronger, opposite force prevailed, dragging him further from the fence, from salvation.

He looked over his shoulder and saw what he expected to see but still could not believe. *This isn't real*, his frenzied brain pleaded.

He flailed again, and this time spun wildly enough to wrench free, though he felt a sickening tear in his flesh as he did so. The movement landed him on his back, and for a single second, he considered how he might defend himself or fight back.

But there was no fighting back. It was all happening too quick. And the attacker, he realized, was actually *two* attackers. The first snagged his leg again, while the second tore through the organs in his abdomen.

In his final seconds of consciousness, Joel wondered if there was any chance the crew heard his screams over the sound of rain, wind, and thunder.

He thought not.

ONE

Sam Muldoon hung up the phone and called to his administrative assistant through his open office door. When she appeared, he said, "Ready to roll?"

"Ready for what now?" Carly Ellison asked, eyes widening with concern. "I don't have anything on the schedule. Oh no…did I screw up?"

Waving a hand to dismiss her worries, Sam said, "You're fine. This is new. In fact, *breaking news!*"

He waited, wanting her to guess, but realized there was no possible way for her to know. "We're going on a field trip to Prehistoric Park!"

"The long-abandoned theme park between here and Buckman, *that* Prehistoric Park?"

"Oh, cut the fake-ignorant, bumblefuck routine, Ellison. Of course you know I mean that one."

Carly laughed, Sam's worry evaporating with the joyous sound. "Yeah, yeah. But seriously, I'm still confused.

We looked into that place, what, five years ago? I thought it was off limits."

"Ah," Sam said, leaning over his desk and raising a pointer finger, "Yes it *was* off limits. Until this morning. I just got off the phone with my pal Clark, over at—"

"At Priority Bank? Clark Edwards? Tell me you're joking about this 'pal' thing. Since when were you two still 'pals'?"

He shrugged. "I buy him a beer or two about every other month to keep things in good graces. But—"

"So, low-key bribery, got it. Or is it high-key? I can't keep up with what the teens are saying anymore. I try to have my little sister keep me updated on it all but she thinks I'm too old and a lost cause—"

"Will you stop interrupting me?" he faux-snapped. It was playful, though, and he was sure Carly knew it, too. Their banter was the only thing that got him through the long days of the most recent economic recession. "*Anyway*, I just got off the phone with Clark. He wanted to give me a heads up that the Prehistoric Park property officially transferred back into the bank's hands. Missed payments, delinquent taxes, et cetera, et cetera—that's all been going on for a while, and today the bank finally took ownership. Which means…"

He waited again for her to answer, knowing full well she could get this one.

"Which, of course, means there will be an auction. *Eventually.* But you want to scope it out, make sure it's as promising as you think it'll be, then pass some cash to your *pal* Clark and claim it as your own before the public ever finds out it was available. That about sum it up?"

"You always were a bright kid, Ellison."

"We're the same age," Carly replied flatly. "Call me that one more time and I'll 'forget' to make your hotel reservations next time you travel to meet a client."

Sam laughed. He woke up that morning feeling unexpectedly chipper, and it seemed now to be a premonition. Today was going to be an excellent day. "Well, are you ready to roll?"

"Hell yeah, Skip. I used to love that place as a kid. Hopefully seeing it in ruins won't kill my fond memories."

"Call me Skip again and you'll be walking."

Sam followed her into the lobby of Muldoon Properties where she tidied her space and saved her work. They were the only two permanent employees in the narrow office located on the main drag of downtown Linden, but there wasn't really a need for much more staff way up there in rural northern Michigan. They'd hire temp workers from time to time if they were in the heat of a big project, but otherwise it was Sam doing the majority of the legwork finding development opportunities, with Carly assisting along the way. Everything else was contracted out.

Prehistoric Park, now *that* was a potentially huge project, one that Sam could hardly contain his excitement over. If this scouting mission panned out like he hoped, he could turn the couple hundred acres into a prime housing development. A stark contrast from a decade earlier, when there was little to no work to be had within a fifty-mile radius of Linden. He could barely afford to keep the lights on, surviving only off the success from the previous decade before the bottom dropped out. Even then, he might only have made it through because he kept his overhead low, something he hadn't forgotten since, and the main reason why he insisted on a lean outfit consisting largely of just himself and Carly.

"Did you tell Maggie?" she asked, abruptly.

"Tell her what?" Sam chirped back. His face felt immediately hot, like it had taken on a lovely shade of red—like he was embarrassed at being caught. Doing what, he didn't know, and he hated when he reacted that way. But he hated more how much Carly seemed to bring up his wife and the things he ought to say to, or do for, her.

She scrunched her face at his response. "That we're going on this little field trip of yours and that you might be home late? You know how annoying it is to make dinner for someone and they show up late?"

"She'll be fine. I'm sure we'll be back by our normal clock-out time. If things are running long, I'll let her know. Okay, *mom*?"

"Well, what if—"

"Are we going or what?" Sam interrupted. He turned to leave without an answer.

"Wait, is that all you're taking?" she asked, stopping him at the door, the customer bell a millimeter from ringing.

Sam patted his pockets, feeling his phone, keys, and wallet. "What else do I need? I just ate lunch. Are you worried you'll get hungry? By all means, bring snacks. I don't care."

"I meant, all you're *wearing*."

This time he poked his head outside at the wispy clouds in the pale blue sky, looked back at Carly, then down to the golf shirt and dark gray slacks he was wearing. When his gaze returned to her, he was thoroughly confused. *All I'm taking? It's July, if anything I'll be too warm.* "Huh?"

"Don't you ever pay attention to the weather? It's supposed to storm later."

"First of all, since when are weathermen—"

"Meteorologists. And women do that, too, you know."

"*Whatever.* Since when do they ever actually get it right? Last time the forecast called for rain I didn't see a drop. I had to water my lawn extra that week. Besides, a little rain won't cause me to melt."

"I said storm, not sprinkle, but fine. You're a grown man. Which means don't cry to me when it starts to downpour." She pulled her rain jacket from the coat rack, grabbed her umbrella from beside it, and came around to the door.

Seeing the umbrella, Sam's mind flashed to fantastic possibilities, and suddenly the idea of rain didn't sound so bad.

"And sorry, no snuggling up under my umbrella, either," she added, as if reading his mind.

Sam recoiled minutely but thought he hid it well, so he did what he always would in the face of potential awkwardness: pivot and drive the conversation elsewhere.

"Can you lock up? I'll go bring my car around."

Their destination was about twenty minutes away. Not long, but long enough that he figured they could get into a good chat. But no. Carly had her phone out and was instantly lost the second he put his Explorer in gear. After his first question received a simple one-word answer he gave up trying. Recently he'd been noticing a distance growing between them, with their old friendly repartee more often being replaced by a new bland 'professionalism' from Carly. They had the whole afternoon ahead of them, though, hiking around Prehistoric Park, and Sam hoped the resurgence of the familiar banter back at the office was a sign that he could revive the old times.

He changed radio stations at a commercial and got another brief report about the missing kid from Buckman—

almost a month now with no sign or trace—then opted to play music from his phone instead.

Five years ago, when Sam wanted to develop the old theme park land—and found out it was "very much not for sale"—it would have been a gamble. One that, with the benefit of hindsight, would have paid off. But, a gamble nonetheless; there were *still* places in the top part of the Michigan mitten where remnants of the recession reared their ugly heads. Thankfully, Linden and Buckman were well past that, benefitting from the massively inflated housing market—along with the shortage of available houses and land—in the southern part of the state, driving more folks to reconsider life in the great "up north". Both towns were growing faster than their incorporated limits could handle, and with increased opportunities for employment and entertainment in both places, the previously wild and relatively untouched middle ground between them was becoming a hot prospect for settlement. The problem with that area in between, of course, was that it was primarily designated as either State or National Forest, which put a real damper on a developer's ambitions. That is, with one exception: Prehistoric Park.

From his limited research, Sam discovered the land once owned by Alan Tippett—up until this morning—had previously been owned by Tippett's relative. A grandpa, or a great- relative, he wasn't sure. It didn't matter who, exactly, only that it wasn't the State of Michigan, and it was owned by the private citizen before the remaining land became protected. So, in the early '90s when Alan Tippett took over the land, it was still grandfathered (ha!) in, and he could clear, construct, and do just about whatever he liked. And it so happened that what he liked was dinosaurs and theme parks.

Sam didn't need to consult his maps app for directions. Even if he hadn't made a point to do a drive-by of the place every once in a while, he grew up in those woods and knew just about every road by heart. He turned the car onto the east-west Frontier Road, which he knew, a mile down, would bring him to the entrance of Prehistoric Park.

Unsurprisingly, the road was empty. Once upon a time this stretch might have been busy, what with park traffic, but now there was no reason to be out this way. No one lived down this road and it was not a thru-route to anywhere else.

As he approached, his excitement grew. A quick glance in the rearview revealed a grin he hadn't known he was wearing.

The tall wooden gate came into view and Sam slowed, turning north off the road onto the overgrown driveway, then parked.

They sat in silence for a few seconds before Carly said, "Okay, so now what? Is there another way in?"

Sam knew what she was referring to: the ten or so boards nailed across the gate and the chain with a rusty padlock hanging in front to keep it shut. "I've got it covered."

He got out and went around to the trunk to retrieve the tools he kept stashed in a storage compartment. When he came back to the front of the SUV, Carly had joined him.

She saw the bolt cutters and crowbar. "You can't be serious."

"Here's the deal. I intend to get inside this place—right now." He shrugged. "You can either go with me or sit in the car and wait. Which, I should mention that I plan to drive the car into the park. So I guess you could sit out here by the road?"

He shrugged again and went to work on the gate. The old padlock came off easily with a little oomph, fueled by his annoyance at Carly and her reticence. With how much she used to love the place, Sam figured she would be at least a little interested in helping to get inside. That not being the case, he continued on alone. The boards took a little more effort, but each one ripped free with a squeal of nails against the old wooden slats. He had asked her to keep watch, but it proved unnecessary. No cars came or went.

When the last board came free, Carly piped up for the first time since he started working. "Wait. Doesn't that man, the guy who started Prehistoric Park, what's his…"

"Tippett. Alan Tippett."

"Yeah, him. Doesn't he still live on the property?"

"That's the rumor, but no one knows for sure. No one has seen him in over a decade, not since shortly after he shut the place down. But who cares if he does?"

"What? What do you mean, *who cares? I* care. What if we run into him?" She had her arms crossed, elbows cupped in each hand, the signature pose of antagonistic Carly.

"Then I'll tip my invisible cap to him, kindly inform him that the bank now owns the property and advise him to find a new place to be hermit. Now come on, are you going to help me with this gate or what?"

Sam could see her palpable hesitation, but after dropping the tools and readying himself at the left door of the gate, Carly approached the other. With silent nods of *one, two, three,* they both pushed.

The gates slowly swung open. And Carly screamed.

TWO

Carly never would have considered herself jumpy or quick to scream—yet there she was, startled into an ear-piercing shriek.

"Jesus Christ, Carly! It's fake. It's a fake dinosaur. Just a statue. Chill!"

Somehow Sam's voice managed to cut through and she abruptly fell quiet. "Oh."

Warmth crept into her cheeks, then he began to laugh, making it worse. She spun to face him, hands not exactly up as though she wanted to fight, but not completely down by her sides either. She leaned towards him, anger deepening her no doubt already red face. For a moment, Carly was pleased to see Sam shrink back. "Don't laugh at me, Sam. I didn't expect to see *anything* right behind these gates, let alone a huge, *extremely* realistic-looking creature."

She couldn't help the last part coming out with a tinge of sniveling, lessening the effect of her fury, but it must have been good enough because Sam put his hands up. *Take it easy, I give, I give.*

"You're right, this thing *is* incredibly realistic-looking…and it startled me, too. Promise."

Carly relaxed and stepped back from him, letting her face fall slack. She didn't provide him with the response she knew he was looking for, because he knew better. Her moments of embarrassment were no time for laughter, innocent or not. She was thankful it ended quickly, though, and was ready to move on. Occasionally Sam displayed a level of shrewdness, knowing when to not push. It was one of his few admirable traits.

"Any idea what it is?" he asked, pointing at the statue.

Now that she was calm and collected, Carly took a minute to take in more of the dinosaur's details. Standing on two legs, the beast towered over them at somewhere between ten and fifteen feet. From her vantage point she couldn't see how far back it went, but figured its length to be double or triple the height. It had short front limbs, but not overly stubby, and a large but proportional head with two small horns above its eyes. It was a big dino all right, but not necessarily meaty.

She knew this dinosaur. Of course she knew it. Because not only had she visited Prehistoric Park when she was younger, she was obsessed with dinosaurs growing up, and the interest never waned. "It's an Allosaurus."

"Ah. Never heard of it. Meat eater, this fella?"

"Yeah. It's a theropod, like the T. Rex, which I'm sure you've heard of."

"T. Rex? Sure. Thermopod, no. You're speaking Greek to me."

"It's *thero*— You know what? Never mind. It's a big dinosaur. And the question on my mind is why this statue is standing in the middle of the driveway blocking the entrance."

"Oh, well shit," Sam said. "That is a damn good question. It doesn't make a lick of sense. Couldn't have been here when the park was still open…"

"Tippett must have hauled it here after he closed shop to block people like us."

Sam looked side to side, scanning the park and the fence that stretched the length of the property parallel to the road. "Seems on brand if the extra beef along the fence is any indication. That wasn't here before either, right?"

Carly saw what he meant, the steel beams and cross wires and stanchions. Not your ordinary privacy fence. She shook her head. "Not that I can recall. But remember, the last time I was here was over twenty years ago."

"That Tippett. Paranoid freak."

"Well, whatever he is, you aren't going to be able to get your Explorer inside, sorry to say."

"Then I guess we'll hoof it from here. I don't love leaving my car parked in the entrance, though…"

"Hey, wait, wasn't there a trailhead a little way back across the road?"

"Oh yeah!" Sam grabbed her shoulder and shook it gently with excitement. When Carly glared at him, he quickly pulled his hand away. "Right, sorry. I'll go move the car and run back. Need anything from it before I go?"

Carly retrieved her rain jacket, umbrella, and wallet purse, then went back to the dinosaur statue for a closer look while Sam moved the car. The detail was astounding, although right up close she could see the underlying material was—

She rapped a knuckle across the tree trunk leg of the Allosaurus, confirming the material that gave the life-sized model its structure was fiberglass.

Incredibly fine craftsmanship. She wondered who fabricated them. Had it been Tippett? She had a vague recollection that the guy was a fairly well-known and respected paleontologist at one point. Maybe it was Tippett's partner who was so deft at bringing the extinct creatures to life? Carly was only ten when Prehistoric Park opened, much too young to care about the people who opened and ran the place. The dinos held all her attention.

Revolving slowly, she took in the park around her. Despite it having closed for good nearly two decades earlier, Carly was still surprised at how overgrown every-thing was. From the sight of the asphalt drive you could be fooled into thinking there was only dark soil beneath widespread sedges and grasses. She had to step—and not even every step counted—to feel the remnants of the cracked and crumbling driveway surface.

There wasn't much else to see from where she stood, as this part of the park was still well-forested. Not that a forest had suddenly popped up when the place closed, of course, but because the owners had decided to leave a lot of the mature trees instead of clearcutting the property like any other theme park developer would do. *Or like Sam will do if we manage to get this land*, she thought, not for the first time pitting her morals at odds with her career. Leaving the trees played well with the theme, and Carly had always appreciated that about this place, whether the choice was by design or otherwise.

The middle of the road offered no shade, however. A slight sheen of sweat had broken out on her exposed fore-arms and neck. She glanced up and was surprised to see a nearly cloudless sky. It was possible the wind had picked up a little since they arrived, but otherwise…*so much for the afternoon storm.*

Carly wandered around to the other side of the Allo-saurus, hoping Sam would be back soon. The place wasn't exactly creepy, but she still didn't feel right trespassing, even if technically they were only trespassing on bank property now.

Ironically, she'd feel better with him back, which posed another conundrum.

Sam Muldoon, residential developer and expert pusher of Carly's boundaries. If he could take a hint and just let her exist as his administrative assistant, he might have actually been a decent guy. An underwhelming one, perhaps, but likely still decent. Instead, Sam was incredibly pigheaded. And too smart a guy overall for her to truly believe he was simply too dumb to understand what he was doing wrong.

They both grew up in the area and went to Linden High but were never friends or even really acquaintances. Not until later, after Carly's failed stint in art school and after Sam's dad passed away unexpectedly, leaving Muldoon Properties in the too-young hands of the old man's only child. Sam struggled at first, but his cleverness and uncanny abilities of charm and persuasiveness helped secure his first couple big projects. Those turned into successes and he was off and running. Carly was back in town, licking her wounds, warding off insults and criticism from her parents, and in desperate need of work—*any* work. Cue the fateful fall afternoon walking in downtown Linden that led her to Sam's business door.

Administrative and secretarial work would never be her passion—not even remotely—but it wasn't terribly stressful, and she was good at her job. And, she always held onto the possibility of leaving for a better career in the future, despite the fact that she'd been working for Sam for over a decade now. Yet, truly, there wasn't much to complain about. She got paid decent wages, enough to support her single lifestyle in a low cost-of-living area like rural Michigan. The only real trouble came from an extremely regretful decision to let Sam date her shortly after she started working for him.

The fling lasted approximately five minutes, but he never seemed to let it go. This, despite numerous times telling him she was not only not interested in dating him, but anyone else either. She got the impression he thought he could *fix her*, or whatever. Worse, his frequent attempts to rekindle a nonexistent fire continued after marrying Maggie, another local woman and old classmate. Poor woman deserved a lot better than what he had to offer.

Carly wasn't overly concerned with Sam, though. There were plenty of times when the focus was work and their friendship functioned. She held out a little hope that one day Sam might accept the circumstances and let the cordial work friends thing be good enough. That would be fine with Carly. And if in the meantime she had to put him in his place, so be it. She'd done it before and wasn't afraid to do so again. Besides, he had a cocky way of standing that left his crotch comically exposed and vulnerable. An easy target for a swift kick.

She was meandering, mostly in a circle, scuffing the toe of her tennis shoe—she'd put her foot down many years ago on any so-called feminine dress code expectations Sam had—in the ground, uprooting clumps of almost knee-high grass. Her wandering had brought her just past the left gate door. She looked up to scan the fence as it disappeared westerly into the trees, and as she did, something caught her eye.

A white object nestled in the undergrowth.

Is that a shoe?

"Sorry about that."

Carly gasped and spun to see Sam right behind her. "Good lord, you scared me."

He narrowed his eyes at her. "You're awfully jumpy today. Are you okay? It's not, like, your time of the—"

"I swear to whatever god killed all the dinosaurs that if you finish that sentence you'll be extinct, too. And for god's sake, you really need to learn more about women."

Sam waved his hand at her apathetically. "Help me close the gate?"

"Sure, but why?"

"I didn't just ditch my vehicle half a damn mile down the road to leave the gate open for prying eyes."

The logic was sound, of course, so she helped gather her belongings. "Now where? Did you actually have a plan, or were we supposed to just strike off randomly for a couple hours and find our way back here?"

Sam walked to the tail end of the dinosaur statue, excitable annoyance plastered to his sweaty face. He'd changed his shoes to more sensible sneakers in the car, she noticed. "Have a little faith, kid! I've got a plan. Might need a little Muldoon luck, but it should work."

"Care to share, o' lucky one?"

He pointed down the driveway into the park. "Find the ticket booth and hope they still have brochures with a map of the park. They had those back in the day, right?"

Begrudgingly, Carly nodded. That could work. "Lead the way."

PREHI
PA
STORIC
RK

THREE

Sam set off at a brisk pace. Carly lingered behind for a second, then had to hustle to catch up. The only thing dinosaur-related he cared about was whether the statues were all still around. If they'd been destroyed or removed or stolen it'd make his job easier, and he was all for that.

"Oh!" she said suddenly. "You want to hear something interesting?"

"Sure, why not."

"So, I read this article not long ago, few weeks maybe, and apparently there's new evidence that indicates Allosauruses were scavengers more so than the out and out top predators everyone originally thought."

"You still read articles about dinosaurs? How old are you? And in what eon is that interesting?"

"At least I don't play fantasy football," Carly replied.

"At least football is a real thing! You know, happening in this century?"

"Understanding the history of earth is interesting and useful, and besides, dinosaurs are just fucking cool."

"Fine, whatever. When I buy this place, I'll have all the statues sent to your house."

"That would be, quite possibly, the nicest thing you've ever done for me."

Sam grunted. "Sounds like you're forgetting about your annual—"

"Hey, look. That's got to be the ticket booth, right?"

He followed her pointed finger. They'd made it to the remains of the parking lot off to their left, and up along a narrower path was a small building. It was obvious now, as they walked toward it, but they could only have seen it earlier if they'd been paying close attention. The rectangular box of a building was just off the path, tucked underneath and between a few cedar trees. Shrubs, grass, and time helped obscure the once brightly painted structure; the yellows faded to a dingy tan and the reds into a browning rust color. The shingled roof was covered in moss and tree litter, and had a noticeable sag. Fragments of glass along a pair of sills implied the place used to be closed up with windows. But no longer.

"You really think you'll find a map in there? Still intact?"

"Hmm…" His previous certainty had left. "Well, let's find out."

"Be my guest," Carly said. "I can only imagine what kind of critters have made that place a home. Maybe even a brown recluse. Which, reminds me…do you have any service on your phone? In case I need to call for help after you get bitten by a poisonous spider?"

The look he gave her was supposed to read as annoyed, but he couldn't fully suppress the fear. "I've got nothing. Surprise, surprise, another signal-dead zone in the backwoods."

"So much for getting in touch with Maggie then, huh?"

He frowned but ignored the question and checked side of the structure where the door was located. It was buried and blocked by a fallen branch and other debris, so he returned to the front, grabbed a stick from the ground, and brushed the remaining shards of glass from the bottom sill. Once cleared, he vaulted in through the opening, landed awkwardly, and gave a grunt for his efforts, but raised his hands in mock triumph. *Ta da!*

Carly stood watching him rummage. He ducked out of sight for a minute, then resurfaced again to stand on his tiptoes, reaching for a high shelf.

She made a noise as if to tell him to give it up, but Sam interrupted before she could. "Oh baby! Muldoon luck strikes again!"

"You've got to be shitting me," she muttered. But she was smiling, too. "I guess we're really doing this."

Sam set a box on the ticket booth counter and motioned Carly over. Inside were stacks of tri-fold pamphlets, faded with age and wrinkled from exposure, but otherwise miraculously intact. He handed one to her and spread another for himself.

The main page contained an illustrated map of the theme park highlighting the buildings, attractions, and dinosaurs. Sam noted the large pond towards the north end of the park, hoping it could become a feature in his future housing development. Also of interest were the "Sauropod Swamp" and the "Triassic Treehouse," though the latter was for childish reasons—he'd always wanted one as a kid but his father refused. Maybe, finally, he'd get one.

"Okay, so we have a map," Carly said. "What all are we looking to see here?"

"It's more about what I hope we don't see. You know, the usual things that could cause unwanted costs or make this venture risky. If the land is relatively flat with only some dilapidated buildings and random dino statues, no big deal. I think making a loop around the park will be enough to notice red flags."

She nodded along, staring at the map as he spoke. "What about this swamp? Think that'll cause any trouble?"

Sam teetered his head side to side. "Maybe. Depends if it's actually a swamp, by which I mean wetland. And how big. I'm not too worried, though. The environmental consultants we used on the Kingston development were easy to work with and pretty cheap."

"Didn't they recently get in trouble for their… practices?"

He made a *pfft* noise and rolled his eyes. "That got cleared in the court. Besides, no one except the dirty earth freaks care if the wetland replacements are actually viable. Certainly not the government. Just gotta do the paperwork."

"Right…"

After taking another look at the map to memorize a few details, he pocketed it. He climbed out of the booth and dusted his legs and shoulders of dirt and spiderwebs.

"So, anyway, I think we should be good to follow the path, take a left at the first fork, and let it take us around. Get the real tour of the place."

"Good enough for me," Carly said.

They set off due north and quickly came to a three-pronged fork. Just beyond, along the straight fork, was the gift shop. Sam felt an odd pull to check the place out, see what might have been left behind—but no. They could take a look later after they'd scoped out the rest of the park. Maybe he'd get lucky and find a little souvenir for Carly. She'd eat that shit up.

They took the left fork as discussed and motored on in search of Sam's future moneymaker.

FOUR

Friday afternoon and his shift was almost over. He even got the night off from the high school football game, since the Buckman Beavers were away. Sheriff Mike Upton *hated* working football games. Sure, like any other good man's man, he liked to watch sports, but that was limited to college and pros. The Buckman varsity team was a shit ass program on the best of nights. And worse, what really set Upton over the edge was that libtard athletic director—*who the fuck let this guy in?* That was what Upton wanted to know—allowing a girl on the team. A girl? What was next, forcing all the male students to take a baking class? Buckman wanted to play to their namesake, apparently, and not the woodland creature kind.

He cruised the far reaches of the county, window down, wasting time. If he kept driving around long enough—which was part of his purview—there would conveniently be no time left to do paperwork before setting off for home. Recent mandates to prevent unnecessary overtime hours for budgetary reasons made it all possible to push the bullshit work to a later date, the most bothersome of which was the paperwork on the Harding case—a closed case, as far as he was concerned. Even thinking about it made him angry all over again. He wasn't sure his blood pressure ever really returned to normal after dealing with, once again, that self-righteous bitch, Laura Harding.

It didn't matter how many times he told her that her brother had run away. She simply didn't want to hear it and was convinced *something happened to him*. Well, maybe, but he was over three weeks missing now, so chances of finding him alive would be about zero anyhow. What was he supposed to do, comb every square inch of the primarily forested county? Teenagers ran away. It happened. Joel Harding just as likely hitched a ride downstate to head back to wherever they moved from.

Upton suggested to the woman that if she wanted to "investigate" she should talk with her parents. Role models, those two were not, and if he had to bet, they were likely the reason the kid ran away. She didn't take too kindly to that, of course, and resorted to calling him names. Lots of filthy names. His blood pressure rose, his face and neck grew hot.

The final straw had been when she mentioned she'd been down to the high school, talking to the students—

Upton's son included. How or why she thought Damian had anything to do with Joel's disappearance was beyond him—Damian swore he'd never met the kid and only seen him once in the school hallway—but Upton lost it when he found out she'd been harassing his boy. The presence of other officers at the station was all that prevented him from striking the dumb bitch. He almost did it anyway.

Thankfully, after that, she got up to leave. On her way out, Upton told her to let it go and get on with her life. What he really wanted to say was, "Fuck off and never come back."

Upton flipped his blinker to turn down Spruce Road before he fully realized where he was and what he was doing. He should not have been surprised, though, what will all that chewing over Harding, that he'd end up taking a lap around Prehistoric Park. Laura mentioned it during their heated exchange, but Upton dismissed it outright; the old theme park had been abandoned long enough no one cared about it anymore. It was well past old news.

Yet, here he was, driving by.

A car, parked in the grass off the side of the road ahead, stole his attention. *That bitch*, Upton thought as he slowed, then slammed on the brakes. Even if it took a few seconds to fully recognize the vehicle, the out-of-state plates were a dead giveaway. He maneuvered his SUV in tight behind the Subaru, delighted to see there was no clear path for the other car to get back on the road.

He got out and found the other vehicle empty. No surprise, but due diligence and all. Still, he couldn't quite fathom why that woman was so stuck on Prehistoric Park, the fence of which was just visible through the trees to the south.

After a quick scan of the area, Upton paused and drew a deep breath in contemplation. His watch reminded him it was already half past two, less than a half hour before quitting time. If he let this go—because he didn't *know* Harding was trespassing, the excuse-generating part of his brain informed—he could be sucking down a double of Johnny Walker at The Local by quarter after three.

Then again…

Then again, he of course knew she had gone into the private property, and arresting people who rubbed him the wrong way was one of the unique pleasures in Upton's life. He might even go as far as saying he'd receive tremendous joy from taking her back to the station to stew in a holding cell for a while. It wouldn't be long, of course, but any amount of time behind bars would no doubt wipe the arrogant sneer from her bitch face.

So it was settled.

Upton, who fancied himself a damn fine hunter and tracker, immediately sniffed out the signs of her path. Of course, bent grass and broken sticks didn't make it terribly challenging. Once at the fence, though, he wasn't sure where to go next. The structure was not rotted or sagging, and there were no signs of forced entry. Further, the fence was over ten feet tall and there were no obvious handholds to scale it.

Then he saw it, or rather, saw *them*. The rearranged logs from a couple downed trees that were pushed up against another tree…which gave access to a *third* tree, which finally offered a stout branch hanging over the pointed, wooden slats.

All right, fine. If that's how this has to go…let's do it.

The first step he took onto the man-made ramp of logs snapped a branch. He cried out, more in frustration than anything, and was afraid it might be a lost cause. He wasn't about to break a bone or throw out his back just to quench an authoritative thirst. But the next step found purchase and, despite not having climbed a tree in a few decades, the rest came with relative ease.

On the other side, he looked down. It was a farther drop than he would have liked, but at this point his mind was made. He grabbed the branch with both hands and swung down until he dangled fully below. There was still about five or six feet remaining.

He let go. When his feet made contact, he immediately bent his knees to soften the blow. The movement made him lose his balance, and he tumbled into the leaf and stick covered understory. His grunting filled the woods, but he managed to get down unscathed.

Success.

It wasn't until he was up and brushing leaf litter from his pants that he realized he'd missed something important. He turned to face the fence, saw how oddly it was strengthened and reinforced. But that wasn't the main issue; it was the fact that he saw no discernable way to get back over.

"Goddamnit," he muttered. "Well, I better make this arrest worth it, then."

FIVE

"Isn't that kind of odd?" Carly asked, gesturing to a wooden sign. The words were etched, then painted black.

**PACHYCEPHALOSAURUS
THE 'BONE-HEADED' DINO
CRETACEOUS PERIOD
UP TO 16 FEET LONG**

"What makes it odd? I'm sure they're all over the park," Sam replied. They'd been walking for a while in relative silence. Well, Sam had. Carly kept harping on about the dinosaurs that he couldn't care less about.

"I'm sure they are, but this is the second one I've seen where there was no dinosaur statue on display."

"Yeah, and there's a statue blocking the entrance to the park. So what? Tippett probably moved these, too."

"I guess…" she said. "Still seems weird to me. I don't know."

Sam kept walking. They'd recently passed the treehouse, and he was surprised to see it appeared remarkably intact. Although, "treehouse" was a misnomer. The elevated structure was built upon and into a five-foot wide beam or tower of some sort that was painted to resemble a tree. Which, maybe when the park opened it looked like one, but time had stolen most of its camouflage. Much to his chagrin, there was no discernable way up there. Perhaps there was a lift inside the fake tree, but even still, Sam could not see an entrance. Not that he needed to waste time messing around up there. The tower could be demolished with the rest of the buildings when the time came, and that was what mattered, and the entire reason he was here. Not to fulfill a childhood fantasy.

They reached a rare short stretch clear of mature trees. It took Sam a second to realize he was still shaded, but not from the thick canopy above. He looked skyward and saw a low ceiling of granite clouds. And now that he was paying attention, it was obvious the wind had picked up substantially, the tops of the trees in front of them swirling and waving as evidence.

From beside him, Carly snickered. He shot her a questioning look.

"Well, what do you know," she said. "Looks like a storm is coming after all. A little worried about getting wet now, Skip?"

"Oh, get over yourself. I'm sure *if* it's going to storm, it'll be another couple hours at least."

"Based on what?" she challenged.

"Based on…" he started but didn't have an actual answer. "Just—whatever. I'll be fine. And if you quit dicking around, we'll be done before it matters."

Carly raised both hands in mock defense. "Hey, I'm just saying—"

She stopped, inhaling sharply. Her eyes narrowed at something over his shoulder before widening.

"What?" He spun, looking for the source of her alarm. He saw nothing, only more dense woods. He turned back to her, asking again. "What?"

She wouldn't look at him, only beyond him. "Didn't you see that? There was something— Shh! Listen."

Sam rolled his eyes, but he did listen, too. There was nothing catching his ear for almost a full minute before finally, a faint rustling. Something moving through the previous year's leaves. *Scurrying, more like it*, he thought. Aloud, he said, "It sounds like a squirrel. Jesus, Carly."

"But I *saw* something, *Sam*. You know, bigger than a squirrel."

"A deer, then. I don't know. An animal. We're in the goddamn woods, for crying out loud. I'm sure it's nothing we need to worry about. Please, let's just keep going."

Carly hesitated, but didn't respond, and followed after him. *Good Christ this girl is losing it*, he thought. *Maybe I need to give her more time off. Might help her snippy attitude in the office too.*

He shook his head and continued down the path. Right as he entered the line of trees, he heard another noise, and it stopped him. Because this noise was louder— a snapped stick most likely—and was quickly followed by words. Human words that sounded an awful lot like "shit".

Sam froze, quickly holding a hand up to stop Carly. A figure appeared briefly from behind the trunk of a stout maple tree, and Sam had a moment to realize with annoyance that Carly had been right. That was no deer, let alone a squirrel. It had to be a human.

But really, Alan Tippett? Nobody had seen him in years, and at this point it was common knowledge that he'd gone off somewhere else. The property was kept solvent from a bank account that once had a large sum of money but dwindled away over the years.

But, who else would be out here?

A thought occurred to him: *If that son of a bitch Clark Edwards told someone else about this place I'm going to wring his neck.*

No one moved for a time, and all Sam could hear was his and Carly's breathing. *Well, let's get on with it, then.*

"Hello?" he called. "Who's there?"

No answer. Sam paused before speaking. "…Tippett? I'm Sam Muldoon from Muldoon Properties, and I regret to inform you that you are no longer owner of this—"

The figure emerged from behind the tree, not twenty feet away. It was a woman, with mahogany hair in a pony-tail and wearing a dark gray crew neck sweatshirt. From a first glance, Sam guessed she was younger than him and Carly by several years. He knew just about everyone in these parts, but not her.

In a state of surprise, all he could manage to state was of the obvious variety. "Wait. You're not Tippett."

The woman responded quickly, sharply. "What the fuck is a Tippett?"

SIX

The chick was cool. The guy? Not so much. The alarms on her *selfish asshole* radar came alive soon after running into the two. Had to be something in the water around here, based on her limited experience. Laura introduced herself once it was clear the guy—Sam something or other—wouldn't stop giving her the third degree until she did.

She briefly shared her reason for being there, and Carly immediately showered her with condolences and sympathy. Laura didn't expect or want any of that, but still…it was nice. Especially in contrast to the dickhead, who seemed annoyed to be dealing with her, as if they weren't both trespassing on private, abandoned property. *Whatever.*

Just as she thought she was clear to leave them behind and continue her search, the chick offered to help. Laura couldn't have cared less one way or the other—she was used to not getting help—but Carly's offer seemed to royally piss the guy off. And, well, she got a nice kick from that, and so decided the company might be a good thing.

She let the two—*Friends? Coworkers? Partners?*—bicker for a couple minutes, and ultimately Carly came out the winner. The triumphant grin as she waved Sam off and joined Laura's side was a nice touch.

Laura wasn't sure which direction to head—she'd been wandering rather aimlessly as soon as she managed her way over the fence—but Carly had a map.

"So, your brother is missing and you obviously think you might find something here. But why? What led you to the park?" Carly asked before they started walking. Her partner or friend or whatever had offered a final grunt of dissatisfaction before, thankfully, moving on.

"I went to the high school where my brother had just started going and paid a kid a hundred bucks to ask around at school. I'm only a decade older than most of those brats, but I'm sure I look like an old woman already to them. Anyway, the kid came back the next day with lots of random, bullshit sounding stories, but several had a common theme. Kinda felt like a game of telephone. Well, I kept hearing about this Damian Upton kid and Prehistoric Park. So here I am."

Carly nodded along with Laura's story, her expression slightly vacant in concentration. "Upton...Like, Sheriff Upton? Did you go to the police?"

"Of course I went to the police," Laura snapped, then immediately reset with a long blink and deep exhale. "Sorry. Yes, I went to the police and talked to King of the Assholes, Sheriff Mike Upton. Damian's father. Nothing but insults and bigotry. In fact, he flat out refused to help. Said 'teenagers run away, sometimes' and left it at that. Literally never even apologized."

"Oh my God. I'm so sorry."

"Yeah, well, as always I've got to take matters into my own hands."

"Right…so, do you have any idea where we should look? Or, just, everywhere?"

"Well." Laura shrugged. "I parked my car on the side of the road and got over the fence just north of here, so I guess… Yeah? Anywhere. Everywhere. I—"

Her voice hitched with a sudden wave of sorrow. It was one of the first cracks in her mental armor since the start of this mess. She broke down after getting the call from her mom—two days after Joel had gone missing—a quick, forcible sob right in the middle of her bartending shift at the brewery back in Flagstaff. Her boss let her leave for the rest of her shift, but Laura never went back. Instead, she went home and spent the next few days panicking, waiting for an update that never came, until she knew what she had to do. She packed a suitcase and bought a ticket on the next plane out of Arizona headed towards Michigan. She'd done pretty well holding it together since then, not that she was immune to grief or emotion, but because sometimes necessity was more powerful than her own feelings.

Carly waited silently while Laura recovered, then lifted the brochure map and gave her a smile. Laura felt the warmth in it and was heartened again, for the moment. *There* are *some good people in this world.*

"We came into the park by the front entrance," Carly said, "and I don't recall seeing anything—"

The blonde woman stopped, a look of recollection and worry creasing her face.

"What?" Laura asked. "Did you...?"

"I *did* see something. I don't know *what*, exactly, but— But I think it was..."

"Was...what? Come on, spit it out."

"A shoe? Off to the side of the main gate. But it could be anyone's shoe, right? I mean, this place has been abandoned for so many years. Any random person could have thrown their shoe over the—"

"Show me where," Laura said firmly.

They walked at an awkward pace. There was an urgency that quickened their step, but too much was still unknown to warrant breaking into a run.

Laura called her brother's name occasionally but did not exactly expect to hear a response. She had hope still, of course; she'd never give up hope. But she couldn't ignore her pragmatic instincts, particularly not with this lone shoe on her mind. *A shoe that could have belonged to* any-one, she reminded herself.

Yet, he'd been gone for almost three weeks. And the reality was she came to Michigan, and now Prehistoric Park, for a reason: to find Joel. Period. Which, she knew, meant alive or dead. That was why she needed to see this shoe. More than anything, Laura needed some sort of sign as to what happened.

She'd seen nothing else so far. The park was pretty in an overgrown, *nature has taken back over* kind of way. A little creepy, too, seeing the signs and remnants of humanity in the process of being buried. *Subsumed.*

Eerily quiet, too, aside from their slight huffing of breath at the moderate exertion, and the sporadic chirp of some insect. *Shouldn't the woods be alive with birds at least?* she wondered.

Carly cleared her throat, breaking the near silence, drawing Laura's attention. "You said your parents and brother moved to Buckman from Arizona a month ago? That's a long move."

"Yeah, tell me about it. I tried to talk them out of it, but they were dead set. They aren't exactly rational people…I mean, moving *here*?" Carly frowned at that, so Laura added, "Um, sorry. I didn't mean to insult your…hometown? Hometown. It's pretty, and I'm sure it's nice enough, but the reasons for leaving Arizona were so…out there."

"I'm not sure I'm following you."

"Right, yeah, I'm rambling. Okay, so, my parents claim to be 'one with the earth' types. Like, grow your own food, fend for yourself, off the grid. You know? Which, hey, those are fine, and admirable to a degree. And they said they were worried about future access to water—which is why they chose your state—and again, I get it. But, you see, I don't know that I believe they even believe all that stuff. I've heard what they tell others, and I've heard what they talk about behind closed doors. It's not all the same. The stuff they don't mention in public, and save for their private internet forums, is about 5G radiation and vaccine nanobots and fluoride in the water. You want to know what my parents are? All they are is a pair of angry conspiracy theorists. Hell, they're borderline Sovereign Citizens. And they ripped Joel away from his school and friends and dragged him across the country and couldn't even bother to keep an eye on him!"

She was yelling by the end, not intending to vent, but the pent-up frustration and anger found its way out, anyway. "Sorry," she muttered.

"No need to apologize. At least not to me. Although you might want to keep some of that to yourself around here. I might be one of a handful of sympathetic listeners in that regard. Folks bleed red around here, if you know what I mean."

"I do. You can find plenty of those back where I come from, too. So now what, we go right from here to get to the entrance?"

They'd reached a junction in the path. To her left, Laura could see a large building she presumed to be a visitor's center or gift shop. Continuing straight looked like it would keep them on the loop back around. To the right was more open.

"Yes, that's the way. We'll pass the ticket booth where we got this—" she shook the pamphlet, "—then pass the parking lot and soon after be at the gate, and then…"

"Then the shoe."

They arrived less than a minute later.

"Over there," Carly said as they approached the Allosaurus statue, pointing into the tall grass.

Laura took the lead, following the given direction, lurching through the grass toward the fence. After a quick once over and not seeing anything, she began to grow impatient. What was she even doing here? Could this really be the place she needed to search for Joel? Couldn't he have just as easily gone off hitchhiking, if only to get away from their parents? See, now that was the crux of the situation, wasn't it? Her shitty ass parents who—

Suddenly, halfway through her next revolution, she saw it, ten or fifteen feet away.

A single left-foot sneaker. A white Nike high top with black swoosh. It was Joel's, she knew without a doubt, because she bought them for him as an early birthday present right before they moved. When she picked it up, she'd find it to be size eleven. Despite every fiber of her being not wanting that to be true, there was nothing in her mind but certainty that it would be.

A gust of wind met her as she took a step toward the shoe. Immediately, she gagged.

"Oh no. Oh shit. Shit, shit, shit."

Carly came rushing to her side. "What? What is—Oh…" She paused, then said, "Maybe a little critter crawled in and died?"

Laura didn't answer. She had little intestinal fortitude, but at the moment possessed a stronger will to see this through. It was why she was here. Without another thought, she staggered to the shoe and picked it up. She saw the blood streaked across the toe now. She felt the weight that exceeded what she remembered from before.

Laura pulled the tongue forward, then immediately dropped the sneaker.

"Oh no, oh fuck. This can't be real." She made a sound like a whine. Her stomach lurched once but the gag was caught somewhere between her guts and mouth. Her breaths came faster, her pulse thumping away in her temple. She tried to force calm, to convince herself what she saw was a trick of her eyes. When her stomach lurched again vomit came flying out. There was no chance of stopping. It happened fast, but she continued gagging and coughing for a minute after. She'd gone to her knees in the process, and when it was finally over she wiped her mouth and spat on the ground.

"His foot… Jesus Christ, Carly. His foot, it—it's really right here, still inside the shoe."

She waited for the reaction, but never got one. Finally, she realized her companion hadn't said anything in minutes. She turned. "Carly?"

The woman was where Laura had left her, but was now looking at the gate, her face frozen in confusion and fear. "Someone knows we're here." She pointed at the double-doored entry. "Someone came and locked us in."

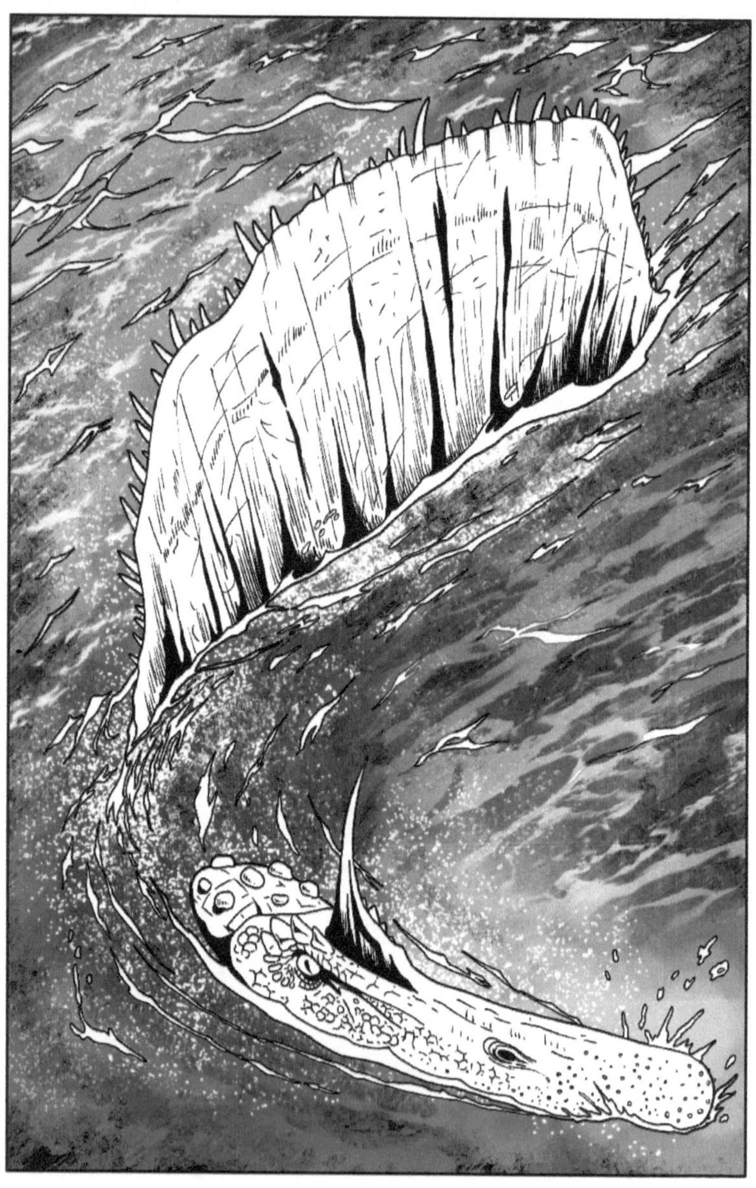

SEVEN

Everything was looking great.

Sam could feel the ridiculous grin on his face at the prospects, but could not be bothered to wipe it away. This exploratory trip was going swimmingly—aside from that annoying woman causing drama and distracting Carly—and by his rudimentary estimations, he was going to make a pretty penny flipping this property into a prime residential development.

He wasn't seeing much as he walked through the park, and that was exactly what he'd hoped for. He realized too late that he'd missed the swamp thanks to Laura's intrusion, but it had to have been about where she came in from the woods, and so he figured it couldn't have been bad if she got through unscathed. Then there looked to be a dinosaur statue in the pond—at least he assumed the spiny-looking fan sticking out of the water was from a dino—and that would be a little more work to extract, but really not bad at all. And, sure, he'd have to clear cut a hell of a lot of trees, but he could turn around and sell all the timber to the locals, what with outdoor boilers being a common heating method in these hinterlands. Not Sam, though, God no. He lived close to town for many a reason, and one of those was access to cheap and easy natural gas.

There was evidence of the tracks indicated on the map for some kind of tram or trolley, though they were at least partially ripped out—and wouldn't be cause trouble anyway. Even the relative grade of the land was in his favor. He hadn't noticed much of any change in elevation in all the areas he'd walked, and anything that did look hilly seemed to exist on the periphery of the property.

So, yes, all in all, prospects were grand. Sam only had a small section of path left to traverse to get back to the fork by the gift shop and main drag into the park. Unless he happened upon a massive pit or a random sign indicating a stock of buried radioactive material, he had every intention of leaving this place ecstatic and calling Clark Edwards the moment he regained cell service to put in his offer. Not that there needed to be much negotiation. Sam had done his homework and Clark was loose-lipped on the info; the number the bank expected was reasonable enough for Sam to pull the trigger without a second thought.

"Goddamn, what a day!" he exclaimed, scaring a couple birds into flight. He created a fake rifle with both hands and pretended to shoot them out of the air. *Pew pew.*

He stared after the birds while he walked, and when he brought his gaze level again he'd reached a corner. Looming just around the bend was a massive dino statue that pulled a yip from his next exhale and turned his grin into a flash of a frown.

"Damn blasted sonofagoddamn bullshit monster," he said, though more annoyed at himself for being spooked by an inanimate sculpture, regardless of how lifelike it looked. Sam refused to let it ruin his good mood, though. He glanced up at the dinosaur again—

Surely this one is a T-Rex? It looks an awful lot like that ugly, snaggletoothed beast chasing the Jeep in that old movie.

—its head bent low as if searching for something. Even still, Sam would have to jump to touch the bottom jaw. The animal's left eye was missing in favor of a blasted out (*or blasted in?*) hole in the fiberglass structure. Seeing that deformity, Sam looked closer and found a deep gouge in the near leg and a couple missing claws on one hand. *Or is it paw? Who the fuck knows,* he thought.

"Carly would know," he admitted. "You've seen better days, huh, pal? Well, give me a couple months and I'll put you out of your misery."

As if inadvertently summoning his own chance at misery, Sam felt back to back drops of rain, one on his arm and the other on his face. He left the T-Rex behind, fore-going a walking pace in favor of a light jog. No matter what he said to Carly about his weather assurances, he wasn't taking any chances and had zero intention of getting caught in a downpour. He checked his watch as he went, seeing he'd get back to the gate a few minutes before he told Carly to meet him. He hoped she was there and ready to go, but if not, he would probably jog right on out to his SUV. Carly could wait in the rain for him to come back; she was prepared for that apparent inevitability.

The first roll of thunder reached his ears, much closer and louder than seemed to make sense. Had he somehow missed the more distant rumbles before now? Or was the sound amplified by a carrying wind that had noticeably quickened in the preceding minutes?

The jog became a run and soon the fork was in sight. He hooked a left without hardly slowing and sped on. The *allo-whatsis* dinosaur came into view, then he saw Carly, her back to him. Her blonde hair was beginning to darken with the rain, which was too bad, and worse, she was still with that angry, smug woman. His immediate annoyance at see-ing Laura morphed suddenly into confusion at noticing them huddled on the ground against the closed gate.

His stomach felt weighted by a stone of unease, which served to slow his step until he was walking again upon approach. The rain hadn't hit full on, but steady drops plinked against his skin, his polo starting to cling. A stolen glimpse above confirmed slate, ominous clouds stretching far beyond the visible horizon. This wasn't going to be a quaint afternoon sprinkle. *Goddamn Carly was right.*

"Shit," he whispered. When he got to the girls he spoke loud enough for them to hear, "What's going on? Something wrong?"

Carly jumped up as though Sam's words goosed her. Had she not noticed him approaching? And was Laura…*trembling?*

"Oh my God, Sam. Something's wrong. Someone—I think Tippett knows we're here."

"Tippett? What are you talking—"

His eyes had been drawn to the gate behind Carly as she spoke, but he couldn't place what drew them there until now. The doors were secured shut again, this time from the inside, with many crossbars and screws. This wasn't a *quick board here, nail or two there* type of job. Even if Sam still had the crowbar, he didn't think that alone would come close to getting them out.

Sam spun in a circle, as though his discovery of the situation would cause Tippett to appear suddenly behind him. But he could see no one else.

"There's more, Sam," Carly said softly.

He ignored her and said, "It doesn't make sense. Unless he doesn't think we're still in here?"

"Sam."

"He must not think there's anyone here. If he wanted to keep people out, then why lock supposed trespassers in? Hell, we don't even know if it *is* this Tippett guy. For all we know he's dead—"

"Sam!"

As if yelling his name wasn't enough, Carly grabbed his shoulder and gave him a little shake.

"What the hell? I'm trying to figure this out. What's your deal?"

Carly pointed at Laura still sitting on the ground. The woman hadn't said a word since he'd arrived. There was a random white shoe laying on the ground several feet away that looked preposterously out of place. He checked the feet of both women, then, because his mind couldn't handle the juxtaposition of the scene, checked his own feet, certain that he'd see the owner of the spare shoe.

"It's her brother's shoe," Carly explained finally, mercifully.

"Oh, you're kidding. So, he was here?"

"His foot," Laura croaked.

Sam made another confused face at Carly, one eyebrow cocked. His hair had flattened under the persistent sprinkling, and now a trail of water dripped down his forehead and into that eyebrow.

She cleared her throat and translated. "His foot is still inside…the shoe."

"Oh fuck me," Sam said, his insides instantly queasy. Broken bones or blood or anything remotely related were a no-go for him. Couldn't handle seeing or really even thinking about it. "We need to get the fuck out of here. Move. Let me get a better look at the gate."

Carly didn't budge. "What about Laura? What about her brother?"

"What about him? As far as we know he is currently still missing." He did not believe that, but he needed to continue thinking about the kid in that manner—simply missing—to keep his head level and stomach settled. "I got what I needed and now I'd like to leave. If she wants to stay here, that's fine. If she wants to go I'll do her a favor and drop her off at her car, or at the police station where she can report what she found. I don't care either way, but I'm leaving. In case you hadn't noticed, we are clearly not wanted in here, or worse, someone wants us..."

He let that thought trail off, not wanting to give what he was thinking any weight. If Tippett—or whoever—wanted to keep them in, Sam didn't want any part of what came next. A possibly deranged recluse like that might have ideas on recreating *The Most Dangerous Game,* for all he knew.

No, thanks.

"Fine," Carly said on an exhale, irritation souring the tang of her breath. "Laura, do you want to go with us?"

The grieving woman stood wearily. "Yeah, okay. At least I have some evidence now for that bastard sheriff."

"Great, we're all in agreement," Sam said, wincing at the now steady, full raindrops that would have him soaked in minutes. He eyed Carly's rain jacket and umbrella with envy. Another low boom of thunder rippled around them. "Move away from the gate. I need a better look."

This time Carly did move, pulling Laura under her umbrella along with her. Immediately, Sam's mouth twitched, and his minutely slumping shoulders betrayed the confidence he intended to exude.

The new fasteners would create decent footholds, but they were all low. They would have to climb up them and still jump to reach the top of the gate. Even on a clear day, he thought there was little chance of accomplishing that, let alone with everything now rain-slicked.

Still, he had to try, right?

Without further thought or hesitation, Sam stepped high on the first foothold he could manage and pushed himself up and into the gate. His initial momentum forced his body against the doors long enough to take another step, but there was no clear handhold beside or above him, so all he could do was squeeze his hands flat and try to wedge his fingertips into the grooves between abutted slats. He lasted another couple seconds before his weight and gravity yanked him back to the ground. In a desperate move, he launched himself with all his might…

And didn't come close to reaching the top of the gate. He grasped wildly for something—anything—but found no place to grip and came hurtling back to the earth.

His back hit first, sending his breath out in an exaggerated *oof*, along with a pulse of pain throughout his body. The hit to his ego was worse, though, and that was motivation enough to leap to his feet a second later.

"Jesus, Sam! Careful! What're you doing? Trying to kill yourself?"

Sam waved her off, trying to avoid lingering on what happened. Through heavy breathing, his mind scrambled for another solution.

"Really, stellar work there, my man," Laura said without an ounce of humor.

"Shut up," he snapped. "I'd like to see you— Wait. The kid. Do we have any how idea how he got in here? Is he some expert climber or something? Or did he find another way in?"

"We found what used to be a hole in the fence near…um, where we found the shoe," Carly said. "But it's been blocked off. Looks like recently, too. I'm guessing sometime after Joel came through."

"*Goddamnit!*" Sam screamed, causing Carly to shrink back like he'd slapped her. A brief zap of embarrassment graced his neural network, then rapidly dissipated in favor of annoyance, anger, and, loathe that he was to admit it…fear. "All right. Laura, you said you climbed some trees and got over the fence that way? I guess that's our next best chance. Let's follow the fence and see if we can't find something similar to get us out. Should we split up? You go east and I go west?"

"No way," Carly said. "If we can't find something soon we'll get too far apart, and we wouldn't be able to call for the other. And no cell service, remember?"

"Fine, we'll go together. Which way? My vote is west, in the direction of the car."

"Sounds like you have it all settled then," Laura responded. "Lead the way, Cap."

Sam paused to glare at her for a moment, but chose to let it go. No time. "Whatever. Let's go."

EIGHT

Carly *knew* it was going to storm. Like it was her sixth sense or something. And sure enough, the storm had arrived and there was no hope on the horizon of a quick shower. It was a curious thing, discerning an actual moment when the storm had, quote-unquote, *arrived.* It had been lurking for a while now, and the rain had fallen for almost as long. That first visible streak of lightning, though, *that* was what Carly attributed to the start of the actual storm. Perhaps, too, it had to do with the ozone smell that her sensitive nose had keyed in on. Whatever the reason, the thunderstorm was upon them, and if they didn't find a way out of Prehistoric Park soon, they might be better off running back to hide out in the gift shop, regardless of whatever unknown threat this mythical Tippett created.

She followed Sam as they crept along the fence, look-ing for a suitable tree or set of trees to aid them in getting over. There was no path or clear way along, so Laura trailed awkwardly, staying under the umbrella as best she could when there was enough room, and falling behind in a single file when there wasn't. Carly routinely had to collapse the umbrella just to sneak through and around brush and trees. Not that any of the trees that were close to the fence thus far were tall enough or had appropriate branches for climbing and scaling it.

The trees were hardly her main point of focus, anyway. She wanted out, of course, and sensed a danger that she couldn't quite articulate or grasp, less so because of the gate being re-secured—which was bad enough—and more so due to the human foot separated from its teenage body. *Christ*, she thought, *what a nightmare.* And while she assumed Laura's main line of thoughts probably revolved around where the rest of Joel might be—and in what condition—Carly was more concerned with what could have happened to the boy to leave a severed foot. It would've had to have been a hell of a freak accident, she reasoned, but one she couldn't picture. *Had Tippett found him trespassing and done more than block his exit?*

Too many questions remained, which meant she needed to pull it together and concentrate on getting out of the park. Sam would, no doubt, cut Laura loose as soon as his base obligations were met, but Carly had every intention of helping the woman get a resolution.

As they left the gate, Carly let the others go on ahead while she pretended to tie her shoe, and when they weren't looking grabbed Joel's shoe—*and foot, oh my god*—and chucked it over the fence. She thought it could be helpful later on but didn't want to bother the already distraught Laura. Caught in one of the mechanisms of grief—perhaps denial—Laura had refused to go near it or touch it again. But there was a good chance they might need it later for evidence, especially if Sheriff Upton was being as obtuse as Laura indicated. Besides, Carly didn't want to have to come back into the park and hope the shoe was still there.

So much for my fun trip down memory lane. This place is officially ruined in my mind. Maybe it really would be best to bulldoze the whole damn thing. She hated thinking it, but there it was anyway.

"Hey, this looks promising!" Sam called to them over his shoulder.

A mostly uprooted tree was leaned up against the fence, the weight of it causing the barrier to bend slightly. Tippett had done a good job fortifying the structure, though, because it did not appear in danger of falling over despite the tree's size.

"Think it'll hold?" she asked as they came up to it.

Sam slapped the trunk and said, "This thing? You bet it will. Look, it still has leaves on the branches. Must've come down recently." He pushed on it briefly and nodded. "This'll hold."

Carly eyed the sheen of rainwater flowing down the grooves in the bark. "It might be slippery—"

"Wood tends to be slippery when wet. It's all about how you handle it," Sam said. He didn't need to wink; his tone did that for him.

"Wow. You're a child," Laura said.

Carly continued on, ignoring them. "And there aren't a ton of places to hold on… This could be tricky. We'll have to shimmy up slowly."

She couldn't hide the hesitation in her voice, and Sam pounced on it.

"Well, do you have a better idea?"

"Jesus, dude," Laura interjected. "Just chill. I'll try it first. I have a little experience, after all."

Carly saw Sam's jaw working in her periphery, as though he wanted to object, but he remained silent. She had an idea he was reliving the utter failure of his attempt at the gate. "Are you sure, Laura? I can be the tester, otherwise."

"Nah, I got this. I'll show you both how easy it is." Then to just Carly, she whispered, "Is he always so aggressive?"

Carly didn't respond, but she wondered the same thing. Was this new? A new level of irritating Sam Muldoon brought on by the stress of things that didn't make sense to the rational mind? She was painfully aware of his issues, but was he always this insufferable and she simply hadn't recognized it before now?

Laura walked to the half-exposed root ball and climbed up onto the base of the trunk. The tree lay at a fifty- or sixty-degree angle, so to simply walk up it was not possible. That didn't stop her from trying, however. Her first two steps were surprisingly stable, but the third slipped and she fell into the rough bark with a soft grunt. She wrapped her hands around the trunk and looked to Carly with a smile. "See? Easy."

Carly giggled, glad to see the other woman wasn't completely down and out from their grisly discovery.

Returning to the task at hand, Laura slowly reached hand over hand and pulled herself along, dragging her front roughly across the bark, seemingly unconcerned with what it might be doing to her clothing. They were all damn-near soaked at this point, even Carly despite the umbrella. Traipsing through tall, wet vegetation had a way of spreading the love.

Halfway up the tree, right as Carly was beginning to think this, in fact, might work, Laura stopped. She cocked her head, looking slightly behind her to the northwest.

"What is it?" Sam asked.

She held up a hand, slowly closing it into a fist save for the index finger, now pressed against her lips. "Did you hear that?"

"Hear *what?*" Sam asked. "I hear pouring rain and trees being whipped into a frenzy by the wind. And thunder. Was it thunder you heard?"

"No, I know what thunder sounds like. I'm not a moron," she retorted. Sam threw his hands up at that. "It sounded like a…a bellow? I don't know. Like an animal of some kind."

Laura watched the woods for another few seconds, shook her head, and returned to shimmying up the tree. She made it maybe three feet closer to the fence—still several feet away—before suddenly stopped and whipped her head back in the direction she'd looked before.

This time Carly heard the noise, too. "Oh my god. What is that? Do you think it's a bear?"

"I don't know," Laura said, peering into the woods, her eyes squinted. And unless she had immaculate vision, she would no doubt be straining to see through the darkened and water-logged afternoon, much like Carly was.

"If it is, it's just a black bear," Sam said. "It won't hurt you unless you, like, kick its cub or something."

"Regardless, I don't really want to run into a bear in the wild," Carly said. "What if this is its home? What if that's why the fence looks like that, to keep bears in?"

"Oh please, that's absurd. Bears—"

A blinding spike of lightning lanced through the leaden sky, followed by an immediate, soul-jostling boom. Carly jumped and heard Sam gasp. But it was Laura she was worried about.

With little room for error up in her precarious position on the tree, the closeness of the lightning strike startled her, too, and she slipped to the side. It seemed to happen in slow motion, as if Laura was framed by the afterimage of the bright light. She fell gracefully, though Carly couldn't exactly call it *falling*. Her arms remained hooked around the tree, so when she went over the side she swung underneath, which allowed her feet to come to rest not far from the ground. She let go and dropped easily to the ground in a firm standing position.

Carly was surprised enough that she felt the urge to cheer.

Then Laura made eye contact, wide orbs of fear. She spoke in a stilted, hoarse manner: "Run."

"Run?"

"Bear! Run!"

"Hey, wait a—" Sam started, but there was no waiting for Laura.

She leaped between them and took off without another word, back along the fence the way they'd come. That bellowing noise arrived in her wake, unmistakably closer. Carly didn't need another reason. She yanked the umbrella down, folding it in on itself in a rapid motion, and sprinted after Laura. She felt marginally bad that she didn't wait for Sam or make sure he was coming, but then she heard him crashing in the undergrowth, right on her heels.

Ahead of her, Laura burst out of the woods and into the open driveway, skidding to a stop by the gate. She spun back to face them as they joined her, her body shaking from heavy breathing. "Where to now?"

Carly ignored the question, noticing right away the thing that made no sense and could only mean something was *very wrong*.

"Guys, the dinosaur is gone," she said.

"Jesus Christ, you're right. What the hell?" Sam said from behind her, panting between sentences.

Laura either didn't hear Carly, didn't understand, or didn't care. Her gaze was drawn to the woods from whence they came. "Is it still coming? The bear?"

"Laura, didn't you hear me? The dinosaur. You know, the big one that was *right here* about twenty minutes ago? It's gone."

"I don't care about the dinosaur statues, dude. I care about not getting mauled or eaten by a real-life bear."

Carly exhaled noisily and joined Laura in staring into the trees. The storm made seeing beyond the edge of the woods nearly impossible, turning the intermittent browns and greens into a deep, dark charcoal gray. The only movement was that of swaying branches and blowing, swirling leaves. The only noise was that of the bustling wind through the foliage and the pelting rain. Carly watched and listened for a few seconds, then said, "I don't hear or see it. It must have turned back."

Another low call from nearby in the woods came, an immediate rebuttal to Carly's confident words.

"Never mind. Run? I think we need to run," she said.

"Gift shop?" Laura asked.

"But that's farther from getting out of here," Sam whined.

"*But* it's shelter," Carly replied quickly. "We can wait out the worst of the storm. Let's go!"

NINE

Torrential rain. A motherfucking thunderstorm. Traipsing through an abandoned theme park, soaked to the goddamn bone, all because of that unrelenting pain in the ass bitch. And after all his searching, after finally deciding to give up and find cover in the dilapidated but standing gift shop, Laura Harding landed right in his lap.

Figuratively, of course, though he wouldn't have minded literally.

The two other people by her side, he did *not* anticipate. They looked familiar, but the light was dim inside the building and while he caught a good look at Laura's profile, the other two were turned away and he wasn't immediately certain.

The three of them were clamoring about something, talking over each other in a way that left Upton confused. He heard random words like *dinosaur* and *see* and *I can't believe* and, for good measure, *holy shit*. He hadn't a clue what they were saying or what they saw, but he knew they hadn't seen him. Not yet.

"Hold it right there and state your names," he shouted.

The other woman was in the process of collapsing the umbrella when he spoke and swung it in his direction with a startled yelp.

"Easy there, killer, or I'll have to take you in for assaulting an officer. Just state your names for me."

"Sheriff Upton?" the man asked, incredulously. "Oh thank God, you can help us. There's something wild—"

"State your name, son."

"Uh—it's Sam Muldoon. Muldoon Properties? And this is my assistant, Carly."

"Carly Ellison," the other woman confirmed.

Ah yes, I know these two. Linden folks.

"Sheriff, I'm not sure what's going on, but I wanted to be clear that as of this morning—"

"Son, I don't give a flying fuck what you aim to be clear about. I'm not here for you, and as far as I'm concerned, I never saw you two. It's Miss Harding here I'm concerned with."

He took a step toward them and they all reacted, subconsciously or not, by sidling further into the room. *So be it, so long as that bitch doesn't try to book it.* He dropped his hand to rest on the butt of his gun. Not that he expected to need it, but because doing so was a comfort to him. And it usually helped speed the process along with perpetrators.

"Jesus, why do you have such a hard-on for me?" Laura said. "I don't know if you're clueless or what, but we have bigger problems at the moment."

"She's right, Sheriff. I don't hardly believe it myself…" Muldoon trailed off, then added, "We need to barricade the door. Right now."

Suddenly Muldoon was no longer paying Upton any mind, and that irked him. The man scrambled around the room looking for something, though Upton didn't know what. Muldoon spoke to Carly in a hushed voice, pulling her into his efforts.

Oh well. Leaves Harding all alone to deal with.

Upton gripped the butt of his gun, then slowly let it go. "I've had enough of your attitude, and now I've got you dead to rights trespassing. So, what we're going to do now is get some handcuffs on those pretty little wrists of yours and take you to a comfy little holding cell."

"There's no fucking way I'm going with you," she said with a force of calm that contrasted sharply with his expectations. "And certainly not out there."

"I wasn't—" A loud and low noise right outside the building interrupted him as if on cue. His first thought was thunder, because that was simple logic, but it didn't sound like any thunder he'd ever heard. It wasn't important, though. Arresting Laura Harding was important.

He tried again. "I wasn't asking."

With two quick steps, he was able to snag her arm, yanking her toward him. She was caught off guard, but fought back, digging her heels in to hold her ground. Upton's strength easily overpowered her, and he pulled her along as he backed to the door.

"Hey! Don't go out there!" Muldoon shouted from the other side of the room.

Upton saw him coming toward them, saw the look of a potential hero in his eyes. He didn't need that right now—or ever. All he wanted to do was get the hell out of there with Laura in the back of his car.

Fuck it, he thought, and drew his gun. The safety was still on, his finger was nowhere near the trigger, and he didn't even vaguely point it at anyone. But it was enough. Muldoon froze and put up both hands. Laura tugged once more, but went slack when she saw the gun. She'd be harder to drag along now, but Upton could sense the victory in his bones.

Cool but refreshing rain spiked his back as he breached the door and the cover of the narrow overhang. He hadn't realized how worked up and hot he'd gotten.

The sky lit up from a scrawling bolt of lightning. The enormous crash of thunder gave his insides a rattle. *Good Christ I hope I don't get struck*, he thought, then heard another noise from the opposite side. Something between a moan and a roar and a braying horse snared his attention, and Upton whipped his head to it.

In the next second, as his eyes witnessed an illogical image, his left hand fell empty. Laura had finally succeeded in pulling away, leaving him alone in the rain to stare down a barreling beast with a bald-looking dome.

The unreality of the situation left him at a standstill. The creature's—*dinosaur? A dinosaur attacked me?*—head was like a stone ram that crunched several of his ribs despite the bulletproof vest, then drove him several feet through the air and careening to the ground. A yell had bubbled at the back of his throat, then came free upon impact, as though ripped from his body by force.

His screaming sounded foreign to his ears, unlike anything that had come from his body before, but there was no time to scrutinize the oddity. He put all of his concentration into fighting through the searing pain in his chest, catching his wheezing breath, and scrambling the fuck out of the way.

Upton rolled and pushed himself up. Miraculously, his gun was still in his hand. He flipped the safety, pulled back the slide, and spun, aiming at the dinosaur that lurked by the door. Its head was turned to the opening. Something had caught its attention—someone else's screams—giving Upton precious moments to recover.

He took a slow, burning breath to steady his body, then squeezed the trigger. The first shot popped off, echoing peculiarly off the building to his side, sounding liquid, like he was underwater from the rain. The distance wasn't far, either, less than ten feet, so Upton was sure he hit the damn thing. He even thought he saw a puff of—*debris?*—leave the right flank of the dino.

But it didn't react like it had been shot. All it did was bring its ugly, round head back around to him. That sound, a mewling roar, came from its open maw.

"Oh, shit."

The dinosaur charged. Upton ripped off three rapid shots that *had* to have hit the thing, but it never faltered, never slowed. And because he was too busy firing an apparently ineffectual weapon, he gave himself no time to get out of the way.

His right knee took the direct impact this time. A crack like an uprooted tree came from the joint as it was crushed, bending the opposite way from what God intended.

Upton dropped to the ground, landing in a puddle. The gun finally fell from his hand as he reached for his demolished knee. The pain in his chest as he bent forward squeezed like a vise around his heart. Roaring again, the dinosaur demanded Upton's full attention. He put an arm up as a worthless shield, but the creature had, surprisingly, taken a step back. Rather than readying for another charge, its head was cocked to the side, staring at him.

"Fuck off!" he wheezed.

Abruptly, the dino ran away.

The Sheriff hung his head, allowing for the tiniest moment of relief. But as soon as it was there, it had gone. His insides felt like they were on fire, and he knew the pain would feel worse if not for the absolute disaster that was— had been—his right knee. He would be walking nowhere unassisted, not now nor for probably months after. That was, if he didn't die from internal bleeding before he made it out.

Knowing it would hurt terribly, Upton took as deep a breath he could manage, and yelled, "For the love of Christ someone help me!"

TEN

"Oh my God, we have to help him," Carly said.

"Do we really?" Laura grumbled.

"Yes, we do!"

"You did see him try to drag me out of here, right?"

Sam's gaze pinballed between the two women. He'd gone into scramble mode when they first arrived inside the gift shop, trying to find something for a barricade. The things they'd seen…he couldn't fully comprehend them, but his survival instincts told him to hide, and hide well. He barely even acknowledged the confrontation between Upton and Laura. But then the poor bastard went outside. Sam tried to stop him…and well, they all saw what happened in the open doorway, then again through the window to the left of the door.

The dinosaur had fled, and Sam didn't know why, but decided it was likely not for any good reason. And now? Now, he was unsure of how to act. Of course they should help the sheriff. But...but a fucking dinosaur—*statue? Animatronic?*—had attacked him. And before his brain could get completely locked up by rationalities, he thought, *How many more are there?*

He began to speak—though in favor of which woman he wasn't sure—when a new voice from the far back corner of the room stopped him cold. "I wouldn't go out there if I were you."

They all turned to the source, but it was Laura who spoke first. "Who the fuck are you?"

The man stood in a doorway Sam hadn't fully registered before. More than half his face was shrouded in shadow, but signs of advanced age were visible. Sam thought he'd need only one guess: Alan Tippett.

The elderly man held a finger to his lips. He whispered, "Listen."

They did.

Upton screamed for help again, calling to them, before going silent. The rain was a steady staccato against the terracotta shingles, and Sam couldn't hear much of anything beyond it besides a fresh roll of thunder that rumbled in his legs. Except—

Except the thunder kept going, getting louder with time, no longer a continuous noise but regular beats.

"Uh oh," Carly murmured. "That sounds big."

The stranger nodded. "I recommend staying out of sight and not making a sound."

Then he took a step backwards, disappearing into the dark. A metal door closed in his place, the snap of a lock resounding much like one of Upton's gunshots.

"Hey, wait!" Laura shouted. "What the fuck?"

"*Shh!*" Sam breathed. "Come back here. Hide."

He ducked behind a table he'd overturned a few minutes earlier in hopes of blocking the gaping hole of the entrance. Carly and Laura came around to him, crouching low.

"What about the sheriff?" Carly whispered.

On cue, Sheriff Upton yelled again in his pained and panting manner. "Jesus Christ, you guys. Fucking help me!"

Carly stood, ever the bleeding heart. Sam grabbed her wrist, began to pull her—

A great, keening roar disrupted their world. The window rattled in protest.

"Oh fuck me! *Heeelllpp!*"

Sam didn't need to pull Carly the rest of the way down. She came of her own accord after hearing the terrible roar. The three of them stooped in the ruins of knickknacks and branded apparel. Sam poked his head just above the edge of the upturned table…

And regretted it immediately.

The enormous head of the one-eyed T-Rex filled the entire view through the window. Rain pelted the scaly-looking skin, rivulets flowing from its lower jaw.

Then it was gone, and Upton was screaming, and then he wasn't.

A gristly crunch broke through and Carly cried out. She clapped a hand over her mouth, but it was too late; the T-Rex heard. Its head appeared in the window again, tilted toward them.

Sam froze, but his mind screamed, *It can't see us!* He willed Carly and Laura to remain silent, willed the dinosaur to go. *Please please please leave us alone.*

Wet chewing resumed and Sam squeezed his eyes against it. He squeezed so hard his head began to hurt and faintness washed over him.

After an unknown span of time—*seconds or minutes?*—the feast was over and the heavy thuds started up again, mercifully receding. None of them moved until the sound could no longer be heard.

Sam stood, his knees weak and struggling to support his weight. Carly was crying soundlessly, and Laura fell to her butt, staring at nothing.

Before he could stop himself, Sam wandered to the window and looked down at the ground just outside. His stomach clenched and shot vomit without warning, the projectile spraying the already filthy glass.

What remained of Sheriff Upton could only be described as gore, scattered viscera, and lost limbs.

Sam spit the remaining bile out of his mouth, wiping his face on the shoulder of his sodden golf shirt. He turned back to the others who were standing now, watching him with shocked and somber eyes. He sighed, reconsidered the words on his tongue, and said them anyway. "I think we know what happened to your brother."

Laura hurdled the table and leaped at him before he knew what was happening. "You son of a bitch!"

He put his hands up in a defensive pose, but didn't actually expect her to attack, and was thus wholly unprepared for the right hook that snagged his jaw. The impact rocked his head back and hurt like hell, but Sam reacted swiftly, fueled by a burst of rage. Catching Laura off guard, he swung his own right arm around, wrapping it around her neck and pulling her into a tight headlock.

He squeezed and felt her neck compress and crackle, heard the whimper. He felt the power in his arm and the control it afforded and—

"Enough!" Carly screamed. Whispering now, "Enough."

Sam released Laura and gave her a healthy shove for good measure. She stumbled but recovered quickly, wheeling around and sending daggers at him with her glare. There were no more words, clearly understanding the importance of staying quiet, and the very real danger Carly's outburst alone could draw.

"What is wrong with you?" Carly murmured.

He waited for the other woman to respond, then after several seconds, he understood Carly meant him. "Me?

You're insane. *She* attacked *me*, in case for some reason you hadn't noticed."

"I can't say I blame her," she responded stolidly.

"What?" He looked from his stern coworker to the furious stranger and back again. He gestured at Laura and said, "She's here to find out what happened to her brother, right? *And* you found his *foot*, for crying out loud. How is what I said a problem?"

"Jesus Christ, Sam, it's called tact," she snapped, shaking her head. "For fuck's sake."

"Whatever. You two can be sensitive or emotional or *womanly*. I'm going to focus on the important matters at hand." He tried to say it flippantly, reaffirm his cool—for their sake or his? He knew, but wouldn't admit it.

He pushed past Laura to the door in the back corner where Tippett had disappeared only a few minutes earlier—though it felt like forever ago. He ignored the disapproving grunts and *tsks* from Carly. The door handle was locked, he knew, but that didn't stop him from trying anyway and swearing when it wouldn't budge.

"You know what doesn't make any sense?" Carly asked. She had begun to pace, which could only spell trouble. Pacing meant thinking—and almost always *over*thinking. "I thought pachys were supposed to be relatively nonaggressive. Why would it chase us all the way here and attack unprovoked? They're herbivores, not carnivores."

"*That's* what you're worried about?" Sam asked. "Of all things. *That* is what's got you confused?"

"I'm just saying it doesn't make sense. That dinosaur didn't act like everyone says it's supposed to."

"Carly, dinosaurs *aren't real.*"

"They were real animals."

"You know what I mean. None of this makes sense. We're trapped in an abandoned theme park with inanimate statues come to life. Who cares if the veggie dino isn't supposed to attack? It did attack, and that's what matters. Not getting *eaten alive* is what matters."

"Sorry for trying to think about this critically. *Sorry* for thinking that the dinosaurs' behavior might give us an idea of what we're up against and how we might act accordingly."

"You're overthinking things, as usual," he said.

"You're an asshole," Laura chimed in.

Sam ignored her and continued. "Well, it's not going to help us. The plan is simple."

"And what, pray tell, is *the plan*, Captain Asshole?" Laura said.

"We're going to block that opening as best we can. Then," he spun and pointed at the corner where Tippett was, "I'm going to bust that fucking door down and find Alan Tippett."

ELEVEN

The door wouldn't hold them for long, Tippett knew. Or, more accurately, the rotting frame holding the door. Finding the entrance to the passageway might take some time, but that, too, wouldn't require too much thought or effort to uncover. There was a chance they'd get distracted by the emergency power switch—the ensuing discussion about which would have been humorous to observe—but they'd get nothing out of it. Aside from the fact that the electrical board there only ever controlled the AV equipment and other odd electronics in the gift shop, its connection beyond the mechanical closet had been severed long ago. All that was left was the overhead light, and that blew when the kid messed with the switch.

No, unless one—or both—of the Utahraptors got to them first, the trio of trespassers would soon be after him.

The man, and one of the women—they had a look in their eyes, less surprise, more anger. Determination.

He waited behind the closed door for a while, ensuring that they didn't err and get themselves killed by the Tyrannosaur, before slipping into the hidden stairwell and descending to the network of tunnels below the park. As he ambled along the underground concrete tube away from the gift shop, Tippett interrogated his motivations.

When he first saw the two on the main entrance security camera after tripping the perimeter alarm, he was irritated. That was his base response, though. He let them explore, knowing their time was short before they'd come to regret their decision. He re-secured the gate, as was standard operating procedure, and refused to worry about them. Choices had consequences, after all.

Then the other two arrived, another unknown woman and that bastard cop, Upton. That was when things changed. Partly because of Upton, specifically, and partly because there were too many people inside the park now. Chances of exposure were rapidly becoming too great. But—

But was that really his motivation?

Important aspects of his life were changing—had changed. No matter how hard he tried to ignore those truths, they wouldn't go away. Was this the reason? He'd simply reached that point in his life where the game became his motivation?

He'd allowed himself the intense and peculiar pleasure only once before, many years ago. A repeat offender who chose the wrong day to steal from Tippett again. That game, and that criminal's demise, were great fun, indeed.

He didn't know for certain why any of these folks were now trespassing in his park. And why so many at once? He could speculate, and maybe find out if the opportunity presented itself, but ultimately it didn't matter. At least, he didn't care.

Tippett reached the first branch of the main tunnel and stopped, considering. He shook his head and pulled the security gate down from overhead and locked it with the appropriate key on his loaded keyring. That tunnel led to the southeast toward an area that never got developed for the park. It was heavily wooded, and for some reason the triceratops liked to hang out there. But no, none of that would provide much for the game. Better to funnel them further along.

Survival, that was the key to the game, right? The key to life? Tippett always thought so, but he questioned that instinct now. Certainly his guests would think so, and the irony of their unexpected and illogical situation was that if they hunkered down and stayed quiet for—

He checked his watch again and did the math.

—another few hours, then almost assuredly they'd survive. But their minds were reeling, resisting this new reality, and Tippett's appearance created enough intrigue, provided a possible answer to the new questions—they would follow him down.

He felt the skin pulling up at the corners of his mouth, a rare smile. *Ah yes, I am enjoying this. The game. This is my motivation.*

His smile faltered briefly as an intrusive thought poked through: *Have I really fallen so far?*

Tippett shook his head of the unwanted conscience and plodded along. He stopped once more to lock the gate on another branch leading to the west, but soon came upon the fork he wanted to take. The left one, bearing northwest, led to the treehouse, his destination.

Thankfully, he had gone through the extra work of adding security gates at every possible branch—just in case one of the dinosaurs managed to find its way into the tunnel system—which allowed him to block off the northeast path and steer his pursuers where he wanted.

Before walking on, he paused and listened. Utter silence. The trespassers hadn't breached the passageway yet. But he couldn't hear the storm either, though he knew it raged on some twenty feet above his head. Those tunnels were a concrete tomb. There was a time when it made him nervous to be down there, his palms sweaty and heart begging to bump out of rhythm. But no longer. There were no demons or ghosts waiting around corners; Tippett had faced them all down years ago. Now all he feared was losing the sharpness of his mind, of forgetting to respect the dinosaurs…

Now, Tippett feared he'd forgotten how to enjoy life.

The stretch of tunnel before him wasn't long. He reached the end of the straightaway in a minute, then climbed a set of stairs that rose back toward the surface. The stairs ended at a trapdoor, of sorts, situated above his head. He pushed it open as he took the final steps and climbed the metal-rung ladder set into the wall, and let it fall flat on the ground before him.

He climbed out into the wide, tall tower, and replaced the door covering the stairs, but did not lock it. Tippett wanted the three followers to make it this far. The next part of his plan, rudimentary and on-the-fly that it was, required a bit of luck, but there wasn't much more he could do to force the desired result. That was just fine. Surprise was part of the fun.

He went to the cage lift and hopped inside. This would take him up the thirty feet to the back entrance of the tree-house, where he could lock the lift and prevent it from being called back down. The only way out from down below was to leave through the door set in the curved wall of the fake tree tower.

The cage rattled as it ascended, the metallic reverber-ations rivaling the howling wind and rain beating on the painted sheet metal walls surrounding him. At the top of its ascent, the cage passed through a floor and entered a small room. Tippett disembarked, locked the lift in place, then exited the room into the treehouse.

All he left to do now was wait for the fun to start.

TWELVE

As it turned out, the door gave way much easier than Carly expected. A few choice kicks from Laura and her thick-soled boots did the job. Meanwhile, Sam snuck outside to retrieve Sheriff Upton's handgun and cover the entrance with the upturned table, reinforcing it with all the junk they could pile against it.

The back-corner metal door gave way to a much smaller mechanical room, which was closed off. Sam began cussing when it became clear Tippett had vanished, stamping and huffing and puffing. Despite their predicament, Carly laughed when Laura scolded him.

"There's obviously another door in here somewhere, hidden. The guy didn't vanish into thin air, you absolute grown-ass child."

Sam shot her his patented *Don't you tell me what to think* look, which only served to make Carly laugh harder. He really was a giant man-child, too full of himself and not used to being put to task. Laura didn't give a shit, clearly, despite their earlier encounter, and Carly admired her for it.

"Fine, be my guest." He stomped out, brushing past Carly to sulk by the window.

Laura was left in the room by herself and immediately went to work searching every nook and cranny. Carly wanted to help her but decided to stay out of her way and wait until she exhausted her search.

While she waited, Carly's eye caught the shelves of dinosaur figurines left to decay. There were little placards for nearly twenty different dinos, but only a handful remained. She was bummed to see the figurine for her favorite dinosaur, the Stegosaurus, was gone. She'd asked for one the last time she came to Prehistoric Park as a kid. Her mother reluctantly agreed, but made her wait until they were on their way out of the park at the end of the day. A return visit to the gift shop never came, either by mistake or parental design. When Carly realized what happened on the way home, she pitched a fit. Mom placated her at the time by assuring her she could get the dino toy next time. It didn't matter, though, as less than a week later, an accident at the park resulted in a worker's death. Prehistoric Park was shut down to deal with the situation and never reopened.

Looking over the rest of the figurines and signs along the shelves, Carly realized all the species shown or listed here were representative of life-sized—and come-to-life—statue counterparts out in the park. Of course, each dinosaur was also listed on the brochure map, but she hadn't given them full attention, rather focusing on the map for navigational purposes. Her eyes widened at one of the names beside the Tyrannosaurus rex. One she had completely forgotten about.

"Uhh, guys? There's a Utahraptor in this park. Actually, I'm thinking there used to be two even."

"So what? There's lots of dinosaurs here," Sam said. "You know, like that big motherfucker that just ate the sheriff."

"Yeah, but the raptors can run faster than us, jump higher than us, and rip us apart with the huge claws on their feet. And while they're not T-Rex size, they're still bigger than us."

Laura poked her head out into the main room. "Another scary dinosaur that will probably kill us all? Got it."

"But—"

"Oh, and I found the hidden passageway. We've got stairs, my dudes," she said. "I'm going down. Are you coming?"

"I don't know, guys," Carly said. "Are we sure this is what we want to do? What if we just hide out for a while instead? Or brainstorm how to get over the fence?"

They'd argued about it all already, but it felt wrong and backwards to be chasing after Tippett. The guy clearly wanted to be left alone. She knew what the other two were going to say, though.

"Carly, I told you. We need—"

"To track Tippett down because he *probably*,"—she said this last word in exuberant air quotes—"brought the dinosaurs to life or turned them on our whatever the fuck you think he did to them. And you"—she pointed at Laura, whose mouth was caught hanging open—"are convinced he knows what happened to Joel. Which, okay, yeah. I can see that."

Carly waited a second to see if they would say anything, and when they didn't, when they simply stared at her, waiting for her to either continue or pull her shit together, she said, "Fine. Let's go."

Laura shrugged and ducked out of sight, presumably down the stairs of the passageway. Sam took one last look out the window, then hustled into the room next, practically shoving Carly back as he went. By the time she entered the small room—for the first time—they were both headed down the stairs.

"Hey, wait a second."

The two paused and looked back at her.

"Didn't you guys see this electrical board? There's an 'Emergency' switch glowing red. It's turned to 'on'."

"I saw it," Sam acknowledged. "So what?"

"So," she said, drawing it out, "Tippett was hiding in here when we all got to this building. *And* you're convinced he has something to do with these dinosaurs attacking us. What if this switch is what he flipped to turn them on, if they are in fact controlled in such a manner?"

"I don't know, that sounds kind of crazy to me. Why would he flip it, then leave?" Laura asked.

"Because he's cocky," Sam said through gritted teeth. "Good thinking, Carly. I say we turn it off. What's the worst that could happen?"

Carly considered the possibilities for a few seconds. As far as she thought, the power was off already. They didn't need power to get out of here. They needed to climb over a damn wall and not get eaten by dinosaurs in the process. "Well, should I turn it off?"

"Yes. Or I will," Sam said, eagerness dripping from his words.

"It's fine, I got it."

Her hand hovered over the switch, shaking slightly. Why was she so nervous? Before she could think too long on the matter, she grabbed the handle and threw it down.

She held her breath, waiting.

And nothing happened.

"Now what?" Laura called from within the stairwell.

"Do you think it worked?" Carly said. "Like, turned the dinos off?"

"I guess we won't know until we see one," Sam said. "And I don't really want to waltz out into the storm and invite one to attack. I say the plan remains. If what you did worked, then great. I'd still like for that old bastard to answer some of my questions."

"And I can't change your mind, right?"

"That's right," he said.

She tossed her hands in the air, then pointed toward the stairs and whatever lay waiting for them underground, as if to say, *well, let's go.*

The stairs descended two stories, where they leveled out into a concrete tunnel. Fluorescent lights hung from the low ceiling—about a foot or two above their heads at regularly spaced intervals. Along the sides and corners were ducts and tubes for carrying utilities.

Carly couldn't see how far the tunnel went, but it all went straight ahead. She didn't like bringing up the rear, and found herself constantly looking over her shoulder, whether it was for Tippett or dinosaurs, she didn't know. In either case, she grabbed Sam's shoulder and pulled him back, leapfrogging him in their slinking conga line.

They came to a section of inky darkness, at first glance a sort of optical illusion, a defier of rationality. Because, as they neared, Carly *could* see illumination beyond. Yet, the heaviness with which the shadow settled upon the concrete they traversed felt excessive and sinister. She had no doubt that the culprit was merely a burned-out lightbulb, but there, the surroundings tickling at the periphery of her senses since they descended suddenly felt amplified. The staccato drip of water somewhere commingled with the thumps of their steps, the resultant echo seeming to linger a beat too long. The musty air that had reminded her of nothing more than a basement before, now smelled meaty, rotting past expiration.

Neither Laura nor Sam lost a step, though, forcing Carly to keep pace, and just as soon as the darkness came, the next working light blew it to smithereens. A bubbling giggle burst in the back of her throat, a pressure release of acute fear. The situation they found themselves in was far from good, but there was no need to get in her own head like that, inventing monsters in the shadows. Dinosaurs were enough.

A minute later, they arrived at the first diverging tunnel. Laura slowed briefly, but the security gate pulled down in front of the entrance, like those guarding a storefront in a shopping mall, left little choice to continue. Carly paused longer, but there was nothing to see. Just another long concrete tunnel lit with more fluorescent light banks. She sped up to catch Laura, ignoring Sam's frustrated, *come-on-move-along* breathing.

When the next security gate and corridor came into view, she did not expect Laura to break stride. A cursory glance to the woman's left, though, resulted in a skidding halt. Carly stopped abruptly too, causing Sam to bump into her and mutter a half-hearted apology.

"What is it?" Carly asked as she came to the gate beside Laura. She hadn't needed to ask, though, because the answer was obvious.

This entryway didn't open into another tunnel. Rather, it was a security camera room. Rows of monitors glowed in the dark, each one showing a different picture, though they were all clearly depicting various spots around the park.

Sam squeezed in next to them and after a moment said, "Son of a bitch has been watching us the whole fucking time."

Immediately after, Carly found the monitor showing the main entrance. "I can't believe it," she whispered.

"Well, all the more reason to find Tippett and wring his neck," Sam growled. "Come on, let's keep going."

But Laura didn't budge.

"Hello? Earth to Laura," Sam said in his most grating voice.

"Do—" she started, then paused to clear her throat. "Do you think he has footage of Joel? Of what…what happened to him?"

Carly inhaled quickly, a light gasp. She hadn't thought of that, but it made sense. If she were in Laura's position, would she want to see that? On the one hand, closure, but on the other…

"Probably, but we can't get in there," Sam responded. His voice was flat and hard now. "Security gate and all, you know?"

"Sam," Carly said, though she didn't know why she was constantly trying to mother him. Probably because she felt embarrassed of and for him. And like her connection to him somehow made her responsible for his horrendous behavior. But she finally had enough of his selfish bullshit. Frankly, she could no longer comprehend how or why she ever tolerated him in the first place. At best, he was an asshole. And if they ever got out of the park, Carly promised herself a career change would follow.

"For Christ's sake. All I'm saying is this is a waste of time. Once we find Tippett we can ask him to show us the footage or force him to or whatever. I don't give a shit either way. Laura can come back with the police *once we get out of here.*"

Carly made a noise as if to refute, but was interrupted by Laura. "No, he's right. *This time.* We should keep going."

Further down they came across another tunnel gated off like the first.

"Anyone else getting the vibe that we're being funneled through here… intentionally?" Carly asked.

"Yeah, I've noticed. But where?" Laura responded.

"It doesn't matter," Sam said. "Not as long as Tippett is at the end of the line. But we'll never find anything out if we keep jabbering like fucking hens. Let's keep moving."

"Oh, fuck off, dude," Laura said.

In a minute they reached a dead end of sorts. The main tunnel became a fork of three, one with a short tunnel continuing straight that appeared to open up into living quarters at the center.

"Holy shit," Sam said as they came to a stop. "So this is where he lives, huh? I'll be damned."

They couldn't see much, but the dimly lit room behind the security gate contained an entryway, like a mudroom in a regular home. Beyond, though mostly obscured, there appeared to be a kitchen table and chairs.

"All this time," Carly whispered, "he was hiding out down here."

"Do you think he's in—" Laura began.

"Hey, Tippett! Come on out of there. We've got questions for you!" Sam yelled, his voice echoing along the concrete halls.

Carly flinched and glared at him. He shrugged, smiling after several seconds of no response.

"What?" he said. "No point going down the other tunnel if he's holed up in here."

"And you think yelling at him to come out would work?" Laura asked. "What if he's just laying low in there, waiting until we leave?"

"He could be," he conceded. "But, what else are we supposed to do? We already determined we weren't going to be able to break through these security gates. Our only option now is to go that way."

Carly's gaze followed his extended finger down the tunnel angling to their left, which, if her internal compass hadn't gone haywire underground, would mean they'd be walking northwest. She wondered where it was they were being directed, then remembered the brochure in her back pocket.

She found the gift shop on the map and traced her finger north, in the direction she was almost certain they were headed. She envisioned the random side tunnels along the main route and matched them up with features and exhibits around the park. If she was right about their relative location, then heading northwest from here would lead them to—

"Looks like he's leading us to the treehouse."

Sam, who had jumped ahead to lead the way, stopped at her words. He turned back to them. "No shit? Well, hopefully we get to go up in that thing."

Carly was surprised to see a slight grin light up his face. He looked like a foolish kid and she felt embarrassed for him. "I guess?"

He took off again, going faster than when Laura was in the lead.

A new set of stairs, this time rising up, loomed quickly ahead. Sam didn't hesitate, taking them two at a time. Carly had to jog to keep up. At the top was a short ladder made of metal rungs stuck into the concrete wall. Above, a trapdoor.

Sam pushed through brazenly, followed by Carly, who cleared the trapdoor, realizing she'd pulled herself up into a silo of sorts. Or a tower. The circular metal wall around them was close, maybe ten feet in diameter at most. It was dimly lit from a light high above, and she felt her eyes straining to see her surroundings.

The interior of the fake tree holding the treehouse, she knew. But where to go now? She spun and saw a door flush with the wall, which no doubt led to the outside. There was a framework for what looked like a lift, something to bring them up.

No car, though.

Where…?

Three stories above looked to be a ceiling. No car.

No car. There's no way up. Only out. What if…

"Wait!" Carly shouted.

But it was too late. Laura was through and the trapdoor slammed shut in exclamatory punctuation.

"What's up with you?" Sam asked.

Carly shook her head, already certain of their fate. Sounds of the storm filled the quiet while they waited for her to reply. Rain pelted the tower wall with metallic plinks, followed by a cacophonous boom of thunder.

She spoke finally. "Laura, is that door locked?"

A murmur of confusion touched the other woman's face as she bent to the door laid into the floor and tugged on the handle.

It wouldn't budge.

"Oh, shit," she said.

"What? What's the problem? We don't want to go back the way we came. We want to keep going," Sam said.

"Sure, but where?" Carly said.

"Up—" Sam started to say, but saw what she'd already seen.

He sidled around her to a button that would be for calling the lift down. Except even before he pressed it, Carly knew it wouldn't do anything. The *off* feeling she'd had before was back and being proven right with every new development.

"What the fuck?" Sam said, pressing the button again. And again. And again. Harder each time until he was punching it.

"We're not meant to go up," Laura whispered, barely audible over the chaos outside.

"Nope," Carly agreed, pointing at the door in the rounded wall. "Tippett wants us to go back outside."

"Well, that can't be good."

"Fuck that guy," Sam said. He pulled Sheriff Upton's gun from his waistband. "If he wants to do this the hard way, then fine. His choice."

Carly shrunk away as best she could in the small enclosure, backing into Laura who looked just as worried about their mad companion waving a firearm.

"Jesus, Sam. Watch it with that thing. What are you planning to do, anyway? You're not going to shoot him." She meant that last to be a statement, but she couldn't completely prevent the upwards inflection from sneaking out, forming a question.

Regardless, he didn't answer. Instead, he pawed at the handle with his free hand and kicked the door. The wind ripped it all the way open until it slammed against the outside wall. Rain whooshed in, spraying Sam in the face, but he didn't hesitate. He marched right outside with the gun brandished.

"Sam, wait!" Carly shouted, moving to follow, or at least see what lay in wait in the woods, but Laura grabbed her arm.

They waited, seeing only spitting rain and distant trees blowing in the wind.

Then Sam screamed.

THIRTEEN

When the door flew open at the base of the tree tower, Alan Tippett felt a surge of optimistic glee from his covered perch in the treehouse. The man of the group of trespassers came bursting out into the storm, gun drawn. *Much bravado,* he thought. But he wasn't sure what the two women were going to do. The plan—not that he really had a plan—worked better if they all stumbled foolishly into the proverbial dino nest.

And sure enough, moments after the man got his surprise visit from the Stegosaurus lurking nearby, they came running out to help.

Noble, he thought. *But stupid.*

As if to punctuate their action and his thoughts, a gust of wind snagged the door and slammed it closed behind them. *Soon they're going to realize the door is—*

The blonde woman spun around and yanked on the handle, but of course, the door did not budge. The other woman noticed the discovery and immediately backed into the wall of the tower alongside the blonde.

Meanwhile, the man was rooted to the ground about fifteen feet away, either in fear or, perhaps, the ill-informed assurance that not moving would mean the dinosaur wouldn't see him.

The Stegosaurus bellowed and took its first step toward him, the man panicked and started ripping off shots.

Bang. Bang Bang. Bang bang bang.

Six shots and no success. The dino, while somewhat hesitant now, continued its approach. The bullets, as Tippett knew they would be, were ineffectual. He might have seen a chip of the dinosaur's animated stone exterior fling off from one of the plates on its back, along with a few other fresh gouges in the 'skin' of the creature; but the only thing that gun did for the man was lessen the time he had to retreat.

Steggy's angry now.

"You might want to run, son!" Tippett called cheerfully. "She's not too happy with you."

Three heads snapped up to his position, noticing him for the first time. He expected the surprise and fear painted on the faces of the women. He hadn't expected the man to point and shoot at him the next second.

Tippett ducked, hearing the bullet wing wide, striking something above and away with a metallic pop. The guy hadn't taken even a fraction of a second to accurately aim, but still…

Fucker took a shot at me, he thought while crouching behind the short wall, waiting to see if he'd be shot at again. *Then again, I am trying to get him eaten by my dinosaurs. Fair enough.*

No more shots came in the first's wake, and instead he heard the Stegosaurus keening again and knew the man had more to worry about than him. Tippett risked a peek over the wall and saw him take off, away from the dinosaur and away from his companions, seeking shelter somewhere on the other side of the tree tower. The women did not follow him directly, but chose to run around the other way, creating space between them and the now charging thirty-foot dinosaur.

Tippett jumped up and rushed to follow the wraparound deck to keep track of their movements. By the time he made it around to the other side of the treehouse, the man down on the ground had already turned around, running back, only this time toward the women. And Tippett thought he knew why.

The mewling Ankylosaurus headed toward them confirmed his suspicions.

Countless hours of observation over the years told him the mannerisms of the Ankylosaurus right now indicated fear rather than aggression. The man below was right to run, though he might not realize it was the unseen threat behind the immediate stampeding beast he should be fearing.

He didn't think it was Rex, based on location and where Ankles came from, though it was still possible. The more likely culprits, however, were the Utes—his pair of devilish Utahraptors.

The women, particularly the blonde one, realized belatedly that the man had reversed course and was racing in their direction. *It'd be a shame if he got ahead of them*, Tippett thought. *I would have bet money he'd be the next to eat it. Or, rather, get eaten.*

The women spun and tried to retreat, but the blonde briefly lost her footing on the wet ground, while the other one got a good jump and got out ahead of the man barreling toward them. *Come on, Blondie, I had you pegged as the survivor the group.*

Unfortunately for the blonde, the man had fallen into a one-track mind. Pure, animalistic determination scarred his face, and he didn't slow a bit when he caught up with her. His momentum and flailing limbs struck the woman and sent her sprawling, and Tippett couldn't help but feel a pang of regret. She never really had a chance to test her mettle against his dinos; she was going to come to her demise because of a reckless man. Even when she cried out, the guy didn't stop. The other woman slowed just enough to look back over her shoulder, but the man was on her fast, pushing a hand into her back to speed her along or, more likely, to get her out of the way. The two of them were headed to the southwest, away from the treehouse and away from the immediate threat. Tippett let his attention leave them in favor of the woman struggling to her feet.

In a move that surprised Tippett, the woman got up and set her sights on the west—the direction the man had returned from. He understood the desire to check your six, to observe and understand the new threat from the new direction. But what it did was leave her vulnerable to the original threat: Steggy.

The Stegosaurus keened again, stealing the woman's attention once more, and it proved to be the death knell.

Blondie wheeled around and found the plated dino storming down on her. She screamed and ducked, pulling her hands over her head. But it was no use.

The Stegosaurus pummeled into her at full force. The woman was knocked to the ground and trampled under the broad, heavy feet of the dino. Tippett could barely hear her cry out, in part from the storm, but also, no doubt, from a sudden lack of breath in her lungs. As the dino ran through and over her, he wondered if the life had already vanished with her air, but no. The woman was still alive, and with an incredible force of will and strength, made the worst possible decision.

She stood up.

And the dino swung its tail into her torso, sending her backwards into the metal wall of the fake tree. When the dino's tail swung back away, the woman was folded over it, and Tippett could see two spikes protruding from her back.

Steggy began to trot away, carrying the dead woman along with it, then twitched its tail back and forth to shake her free. Her lifeless body slumped to the ground, and that was that.

Only two trespassers left alive.

FOURTEEN

Sam might not have stopped running if Laura hadn't hissed at him: "*You stupid fucker got her killed.*" Her voice cut through and put just enough lead in his feet to bring him to a stop. He turned back to watch the scene by the tower. Laura had stopped several feet back, also watching as the big dinosaur with the plates on its back finished Carly off with its tail.

He couldn't believe it. Carly, his closest friend for years, even closer than his own wife. He saw her damn near every day, and now she was dead. And it *was* his fault, wasn't it?

Stop it! It was an accident, that's all. She stumbled, we collided. An accident. Nothing can be done now except get the hell out of this nightmare.

"*Oh shit!*" Laura yelped, racing toward him, thrusting his mind back on track.

The ugly beast that looked like a giant armadillo with spikes on its back—the reason he turned back around by the treehouse tower. Laura caught up to him by the time he got his feet moving again, but soon after, she peeled off to the side and leaped up to grab a low branch from a tree. He watched for a moment as she swung up with surprising ease, then tore his eyes away to focus on running ahead and away.

Still, he had to wonder, *Why climb the tree and not keep running?* Tippett. She still wanted to get her answers. Sam had a hard time remembering what propelled him to seek the bastard out, but whatever the reason, it was long gone now. The only motivation he had anymore was to survive. Sure, the storm still raged, and the gate was surely still closed and locked up, but Sam no longer cared what it took. He'd run back to the gift shop and go find that tree along the fence they had been so close to scaling to get out. If he had to stop every minute or so to hide and look out for dinosaurs, so be it. He was getting his ass out of there, because there was no alternative.

Before he made it much further, though, his world filled with light, and the sound like a bomb going off shook his core so violently he thought he would fall to the ground. A lightning strike had hit somewhere behind him, and he couldn't help but turn back. It was too close.

Somehow, between the noise of the hard rain, his feet slamming the ground, and his heart pounding, Sam had lost track of the pursuing dinosaur. The creature was a mere twenty feet behind and closing in.

He pivoted hard and jumped to the side, committing his body fully to the leap and impact. He took the brunt of the fall on his shoulder, a lance of pain shooting into his collar bone as he rolled through the tall grass. Had he broken the bone? Pain bloomed there, and it instantly brought him back to high school football practice when he actually had broken it. Not even in a game, just messing around with his teammates like an idiot teen.

A mature tree loomed nearby, and Sam scrambled to it, ducking around the thick trunk and curling himself tight into a ball, holding his right arm close and grimacing against the agony.

He half expected the dino to crash into the tree and he sat there praying the trunk would hold and protect him.

But it never came. He heard its thundering steps close by, listening in terror as they grew fainter. Sam peeked around the tree and saw the thing had kept on running and would soon be out of sight.

Sam stood slowly, confused. He hazarded a few steps into the small opening, looking both ways as though he were about to cross a heavy traffic road.

The dinosaur had indeed disappeared to his right, to the southeast. The other way, Sam could no longer see Laura.

In the distance was the base of the metal treehouse tower. But there was more, too. Not the dino that had killed Carly; that one appeared long gone as well. Sam squinted, trying to understand what…

Debris? It was all he could think to call it. *What was that debris littered around the tower?*

Without much thought, he started to walk toward it, his curiosity overcoming the pain to take the reins. He took one step, two, then—

A flash of movement caught the periphery of his vision. He snapped his head that way and a weak, startled yap left his lips. Some thirty or forty feet away stood a smaller dinosaur, about his height. It was stationary, facing him, so he couldn't quite tell how long or big the rest of it was.

Sam swiped a nervous hand across his forehead, pushing his sopping hair out of his face as he took a slow step backward. Something about the ferocious looking snout on this dinosaur scared him worse than the big ones. The clawed forelegs hanging at a rest in front of its body didn't help either. Nor the feet with a single, hideously large talon.

Moving like a snail, he continued to shuffle backwards, never letting his eyes wander from this new dinosaur. Oddly, the creature didn't move a muscle—*Do these moving statues have muscles?* he thought hysterically—though it stared him down as he moved away. It never made an attempt to follow or attack.

A low, croaking chirrup came from behind.

"Fu—"

He made it ninety degrees in his turn when the second dinosaur ambushed him. Sam's head snapped backwards as the dino jumped into him, both feet slamming into the middle of his back and riding him down to the ground. The force of impact and the weight of the monster driving him into the soggy ground might have been the worst pain Sam had ever felt in his life. The icing on this torture cake was the snap announcing that yes, his collar bone was indeed broken, if not shattered.

Then the giant claws sunk into the meat of his back just below each shoulder blade and pulled.

Sam screamed so loud into the mud his voice broke and vanished a second later. He tried to rise, to roll, to shake the dinosaur off—to do anything to free himself but couldn't budge.

There was a quick, slight relief in pressure, and Sam jerked his body to the side. Searing pain like a red-hot knife tore across his back and an instant of explosive agony followed by a sudden dullness. His momentum—or maybe it was the dinosaur on his back, he didn't know—flipped him over, but by then Sam realized he could no longer feel…anything.

The dinosaur stood over him, head cocked and staring. Sam attempted to lift his arms in defense, but they wouldn't move.

Oh my god, I'm paralyzed.

The bipedal creature that looked like half a reptile, half a bird, continued to watch him.

Waiting for something, Sam decided.

Between the eruption of enormous pain and sudden, ensuing absence of it—not to mention the absurdity of these dinosaurs in the first place—his conscious mind felt tugged, enticed to slip away into a warm void.

Let go and let God, right? he thought with delirious pleasure. He thought he could probably still scream despite the paralysis, but what was the point?

If there was even a shred of hope, it was dashed at the appearance of the other dinosaur, the first that had caught his attention, fooling him into backing directly into the trap.

Two vicious beasts with their heads poised over him, looking down as surgeons would, considering where to make the first incision. The dino that took him down made the decision by opening up his belly. Not that he could feel it or even see it happen—he could lift his head less than an inch off the ground—but immediately after, both dinosaurs dove their heads into his body and came up with steaming organs, damn near sizzling in the rain.

They chewed and chomped, fought, snarled, and dug in for more, his body shaking with the ferocity of each dig. And yet, Sam did not die. Bleeding out was taking too long, and the most vital of organs were still untouched.

Sam had enough. With the final dregs of his energy, he screamed at the creatures above him. "*FUCKING KILL ME ALREADY YOU COCKSUCK—*"

The dino nearest his upper body stepped on his head and jabbed its claw through his right eye.

Sam felt *that* all right, along with the burst of his eyeball, its juices splashing onto his face, mixing with the rain. Mercifully, he didn't have time to react or scream, because the dinosaur pressed its full weight on his head. For one final second of consciousness, Sam felt intense pressure behind the piercing pain, heard the first crack, then the final crunch.

FIFTEEN

For a second, cutting through the still-raging storm and utter dino chaos and blood and screams, Laura remembered Joel. A blow of sadness and heartache stopped her cold, knowing he was gone. He could not have survived this, she knew, not after considering his lone foot.

Has it really only been an hour since I found it? she thought. *Feels like days ago.*

From her angle up in the tree, she could just make out the long bodies of the two monsters—they looked like raptors, but had feathers and, well, that was news to her—bent over something in the grass.

That something was Sam.

When the two of them were running away from the treehouse and that charging monstrosity of a dino, Laura quickly realized *they* were not being chased, specifically, but rather the dinosaur thundering after them was. She took a chance and swung up into a tree, climbing as fast as possible, throwing herself against the trunk to hide and wait. Seconds later she peeked towards the tower again and saw the two pursuers coming, then splitting off to either side of the path Sam and the armored-looking dinosaur had taken.

Laura heard—more than saw—what followed in the next couple minutes, and she was thankful to not be a firsthand witness. Or a victim.

But now… Now that the vicious dinos were preoccupied with their feast on Sam, she knew she couldn't wait around any longer. She didn't know what, exactly, to do, but she felt too vulnerable in the tree. What if the raptors found her and could jump really high? Hell, the T-Rex that got the shithead sheriff looked tall enough to stare her dead in the face if it happened upon her perch.

Taking care to move without unnecessary noise—as well as to avoid slipping on the wet branches, falling to the ground, and breaking her neck—Laura descended. At the lowest branch, she dropped, and the soles of her boots hit the ground with a liquid plop.

Backing away while trying to keep the trunk between her sightline and the dinosaurs, she realized she'd have to beg for help. From Tippett.

She didn't care anymore about what he did or might have done, she just wanted to not die. Did she expect him to listen? Not in the slightest. But she had to try. If he wouldn't help, then she'd keep on running until she hit the fence, hoping all the while that she didn't run right into the jaws of another monster.

Eventually it became impossible to keep moving backwards efficiently, so she turned and sprinted towards the treehouse tower ahead. When it came into view, she did a double take, skidding to a stop.

"Holy shit."

A few minutes before, there had been an earth-shaking strike and boom, and Laura knew lightning had hit extremely close by. But, beyond being thankful it wasn't the tree she was clinging to, she didn't think any more of it. There was a lot of noise going on everywhere, not the least of which the persistent, heavy rain—or the constant internal screaming. It was clear now, however, what had happened.

The outcome was clear, anyway.

A mature oak tree near the treehouse was struck by the bolt of lightning, and from what Laura could tell, the damn thing exploded. The ground all around it was littered with chunks of tree ranging in size from a few inches to several feet. Worse was the branch snapped from the main trunk, a branch the size of a twenty or thirty-year-old tree itself, that had fallen across the suspended boardwalk connecting the various platforms of the sprawling treehouse.

The boardwalk was split in two, leaving disconnected ends crashed to the ground.

Laying in the debris was one Alan Tippett.

She hesitated for a long second, then rushed to him. He wasn't so much covered as surrounded by sticks and leaves and broken boardwalk planks. Laura pushed what she could aside and kneeled next to the immobile man. His eyes were closed, and between the rain and her own harried demeanor, she couldn't tell if he was breathing.

Laura placed a hand on his chest, the shirt sodden and clinging.

Tippett jerked. Eyes wide and jaw unclenched and ready to scream. But she acted fast and placed her free hand over his mouth. "*Shh.*"

Thankfully, recognition and a measure of calm replaced surprise and terror, and the man settled. He groaned as Laura gave him space. When he tried to sit up, she said, "Whoa, hold on. Are you hurt? Should you move?"

He continued to rise, waving her off. "My entire body hurts, but that's been the case for years." He groaned again, but in direct contradiction said, "I'm fine."

"How on earth are you fine? How are you not *dead?*"

Tippett stared at her for a moment, his eyes crinkling as they softened. He offered her a wry smile. "I guess I survived so this earth could show me a worse time."

"How nihilistic of you," she said, shaking her head. "Can you stand? We really need to find shelter. There's two—"

"My Utahraptors, yes. I saw them."

"Then you know we can't sit around and wait for them to mosey our way."

Laura extended her hand and Tippett grabbed it. She pulled him to his feet but remained at the ready, sure she would discover he had a broken leg or something and he'd topple right over. But he kept his balance, swaying only slightly, and seemed, for some miraculous reason, no worse for the wear.

"Thank you," he said. "You're helping me…why? I tried to get you killed by my dinosaurs. Why even approach me? What makes you think I will help you now?"

She bit back the retort itching to come out: *You don't seem to be strolling down easy street yourself, asshole.* But this *was* his home turf. His actual home, for decades. She had no clue what safety measures or other secrets he may have up his sleeve. So, she said, "I don't have much choice other than to run wild through the woods, and my luck so far doesn't have me feeling like that's a good idea. If you want me to beg, I won't. But I could use your help."

"Fair enough. The best place to hide out is the—"

Tippett patted his pockets before slowly raising his head to meet Laura's eyes. She saw fear there, for the first time, and that scared the hell out of her.

"Oh, fucking hell," he said. "I lost my keys. So the tower is out. Shit."

"You're kidding."

He shook his head and his tongue darted out to lick his lips despite the seemingly never-ending rain.

"Well, where the fuck do we go now?"

Laura glanced over her shoulder while the old man thought, his eyes darting every which way. She didn't see any dinosaurs, thank god, but in the back of her mind she couldn't help but picture the stealthy way the two raptors had split up and ambushed Sam.

"Come on, man. Where do we go?"

"Ah! The terrarium building. It's the next closest structure we'll be able to get into."

"Which way?"

Tippett pointed behind her—to the north and east, if she had her bearings straight—then shuffled past her, not walking but not jogging either. Laura caught up easily, feeling like the pace was painfully slow, but decided there wasn't much more she could do.

They had to skirt the downed branches and board-walk, but soon found the walking path and followed it toward where she ran into Carly and Sam. Now that they were moving in that direction, she remembered the structure along the path that had to be what Tippett was referring to. Laura glanced over her shoulder constantly, sure that a dinosaur would jump out at any second. The old man looked around warily, as well, but seemed altogether less concerned. She had so many questions for the guy now that she was near him and he appeared to be somewhat cooperative, but she didn't dare speak for fear of drawing attention to them.

Yet, when the building came into view, Laura couldn't help but gasp in relief. She clapped a hand over her mouth, and Tippett shot her a look, but shelter was there, so close, and there wasn't a single dinosaur or disturbance in sight.

As they approached, still a good thirty feet away, a noise snuck through the din. Laura froze, reactively snagging Tippett's arm. "Wait. Did you hear that?" she whispered.

It came again. A faint chittering.

Tippett groaned.

Laura saw movement and threw a hand to her chest to go along with her startled pant. But then she couldn't help but laugh when she saw the tiny dinosaur come fully into view, positioning itself in front of the door to the building. It was the size of a chicken, but a skinny mother-fucker. "That can't hurt us, can it?"

Tippett muttered something and spun, looking around frantically.

"What'd you say?" she asked.

He pointed at the small dino still standing guard by the door, head cocked and staring. "I didn't know there was a Compy left. I thought those guys were all gone."

"So what? That thing's tiny. We'll be fine, right?" But doubt crept into her voice.

"It's not him I'm worried about. It's the big ones that might be hunting it, wanting a snack, that have me… concerned. We're by the pond. We're too close to Spine's territory."

"*Spine?*" she asked.

Heavy, resounding thuds were her answer, and it took her a second to realize she wasn't hearing thunder.

Those were footsteps.

"We have to hide," Tippett said.

The small dino chittered again, louder. Then its noises erupted into full on crowing. They ran toward it and the door behind. Laura tried to shoo and shush it simultaneously, but neither were fruitful. The Compy continued to make a racket, all while the thunderous steps grew louder, closer.

Tippett grasped the handle on the closed door and it turned easily—

But the door didn't budge. Tippett pushed on it, but still, no movement.

"Come on, what're you doing? Stop fucking around." She hissed at the dino now nipping at her legs, "Fuck off, you little shit."

While the old man continued to ram the door, throwing his shoulder at it, Laura kicked at the Compy, only managing a glancing blow that did nothing to deter the creature.

Tippett grunted as he threw himself violently against the door and it finally moved, but only a few inches. Something inside blocked the way.

"This isn't working," Laura said. "Isn't there a window we can sneak through or something?"

Tippett shook his head between heavy breaths, readying himself for another blow. "It's up kind of high. I'd have to boost you."

"Then let's—"

A croaking, crackling bellow introduced the new dinosaur. When Laura found the sound, she moaned. The dinosaur Tippet called "Spine" was *enormous*. It had a long, crocodilian snout and a tall, interconnected fan of spines on its back like a sail. It would have made the T-Rex look small had they been standing side by side.

The monster, drawn by the noise, saw them and charged. Laura judged they had about ten seconds to act. In the span of the first second she saw Tippett still struggling—though finally starting to succeed—with the door; felt the little shit dino attack once more before turning to run; and formed a half-assed, no-time-to-think plan.

She took one step, two, and dove into the small dino, pinning it to the ground. She pulled the squirming, toothy bastard into a tight embrace and rolled up onto her feet to face Spine.

But Spine had its gaze locked on Tippett, she saw, and the old man saw it too. He yelled in terror and threw his arm up as an ineffectual shield, the door nearly far enough ajar now to slip through.

Laura screamed wildly and thrust the frenzied, shrieking dino out in front of her. She had to use all her strength and wouldn't be able to hold on long, but she only needed a couple seconds. Spine didn't respond right away to the cacophony she and the Compy were making, and her heart sank. Then—

The big dino swerved away from Tippett's huddled form and aimed its charge at her.

Laura tossed the dino to the side and held her ground for a split second longer, every internal alarm screaming at her to run, jump, fight—do *anything*.

Spine took the bait and Laura dove to the opposite side toward Tippett and the building, narrowly avoiding the stomping tree-trunk-sized legs of the dino. The Compy hit the ground and took off squawking, the big one giving chase.

Laura scurried to her feet to join Tippett, who had thankfully recovered quickly as well.

Together, they heaved one final time and managed to jar the door loose enough to squirm inside.

Tippett pushed the door closed behind them, careful not to slam it home and risk drawing Spine's attention back after everything Laura had just done.

Chest heaving, breaths in whistling pants, she slumped to the floor and leaned her back against a wall of empty aquarium-looking tanks. She willed herself to take slower, deeper breaths that weren't so goddamn noisy. Tippett backed away from the door with careful steps, and lowered himself to the floor opposite Laura.

They watched each other, waiting in silence, praying the gigantic creature had become preoccupied enough not to return.

After five minutes of nothing but rain—which, she realized now, was finally beginning to lesson, along with the thunder and lightning—Laura decided the coast was, at least relatively speaking, clear.

"What in the fucking hell was that thing?"

Tippett smiled weakly. "Spinosaurus. Only the largest of all known carnivorous dinosaurs."

SIXTEEN

"Don't get a hard on over it, old man. I saved your ass because I still need you to answer some questions."

She said that with confidence, despite knowing it was far from the real reason. Certainly not the whole reason, at any rate. She wouldn't admit it to him, but it was more likely she'd saved him because she'd seen far too much death already.

"Old man, huh?" he chuckled. "I suppose you're not wrong. You can call me Alan, however, if you choose. And for the formal introduction, I'm Alan Tippett."

"Laura Harding."

"Laura, very good. You had questions? Okay, shoot," Tippett said. "What do you want to know?"

She did not respond right away, instead contemplating where to start. There was simply so much swirling in her head. And now that she was sitting again, at a moment of rest, she was shivering. Before the storm, the temperature was unseasonably warm for this late in the year, but the storm front had cut the warmth at its knees in the hours since. Beyond that, she was soaking wet and no longer had constant movement or the immediate punch of adrenaline to stave off the chill. She pulled her legs into her body and wrapped them up tight to her chest.

When she opened her mouth to finally speak, the question, "How?" tumbled out, much to her surprise. She intended to ask about Joel, but her subconscious had intervened. Was it because she already knew the answers? Or because she couldn't bear to hear anything worse than she already imagined?

"Would you believe me if I said I didn't know?" Tippett responded, unaware or unphased by her reaction to her own words. "Not entirely, anyway."

"Then tell me what you do know."

"Yeah, yeah, all right," he said with a sigh. "They—the dinosaurs—weren't always…"

"Alive?"

"Well, they're not *really* alive."

"What the fuck are they? Did I not just see them kill multiple people? What're they, animatronic or something?"

"Okay, fine. I was going to say *capable of motion*, but sure, *alive* works. Anyway, they didn't move at all when we created them."

Laura raised her eyebrows at that.

"Mmhmm. That's right. I was a paleontologist in another life. I knew physiology, the structure of these prehistoric animals. My partner…he was an incredible artist. Together we sculpted all the dinosaur statues."

"No shit. Well, you did a hell of a job," she conceded. "Those fuckers are terrifying."

Tippett laughed, nodding his appreciation. "Thanks. It was important to me to get them right, you know? I mean, sure, I've been out of the research side of things for a long time now, and I know some of what we all thought we knew way back when has since been proven wrong. But I wanted to get them right as much as I possibly could. That movie everyone's still stuck on got, uhh, a few things wrong, to put it nicely."

"The movie…? Oh, Jurassic—"

"Yeah, that one."

"I thought that movie was pretty cool," she said with a shrug.

"Of course you did. Everyone loved it. I'm not saying the movie is *bad*, but they—" he paused, smirking, waving a hand as if to dismiss the thought. He shook his head and leaned slightly toward her. "Want to hear a secret?"

Laura was so shocked by the sudden demeanor change that she laughed. It was like they were, in fact, conspiratorial best friends and not complete strangers, one wanting the other dead. "Sure. A secret. Why not."

"I worked on the set of that movie. I was a dinosaur consultant," he said with a proud, *ain't I the shit* grin.

"For real?" Laura said, letting a bit of exaggerated excitement drip from the words. She didn't *really* care, but it was neat enough and they were just sitting there hiding out anyway, so why not indulge him?

"You bet. Not very long, of course, otherwise it wouldn't be a secret. But I had issues with the way they wanted to design the dinos. Some were perfectly fine, but others? Not so much. Anyway, it resulted in a bit of head-butting and me getting canned and replaced by a more amenable colleague of mine. Bastard." He shook in disgust. "They hit me with a tree's worth of legal paperwork about keeping my mouth shut and blah de fucking blah. Anyway, I told my partner, but that's it. You're the only other person I've told. You're in rarified air."

His smile grew, and he chuckled again.

Laura marveled at the old man. How could this be the same guy that had led her and the others to their slaughter less than an hour ago?

She smiled politely back until he acknowledged it and his glee faded. He sighed, staring down the small hall of the building.

"You never really answered my question. How *are* they alive? Or move or whatever?"

"Ah, you're right. I didn't answer. Unfortunately, the answer is I don't rightly know."

"You don't know? Like, at all? The dinosaur statues you created just randomly come to life and terrorize anyone with the misfortune of being in the way?"

"Okay, I know *some* things," he said. "For example, they don't *randomly* come to life. They change from stationary dinosaur replicas into lifelike and mobile creatures only when it storms. Like, well…like right now. Something about the elec—"

Laura barked laughter. "You're fucking with me."

Tippett's face tightened, then remained stern. "You tell me. Does it seem like I'm *fucking* with you? Really?"

She was beginning to think she didn't know anything at all about the situation. Certainly, she didn't know this man or his drastically opposing personalities. "Okay, fine. Storms, got it. But you said they didn't always do that. So…what changed? How did it start?"

"You won't like this, but I don't know how." Tippett paused, pensive. Consulting memories, perhaps. "I do know *when*, though.

"There was a massive storm a couple years after I closed the park. Intense doesn't do it justice. I remember being at the peak—or pit, I suppose—of my depressive spiral then. I tried to—" He shook his head and started again. "Something outside the realm of what I thought possible happened in that storm. When I emerged from my quarters the next day I noticed my dinos were no longer where I'd originally put them. My first thought was it had to be vandals, or at the very least, someone was messing with me. Not that that made much sense, mind you, because do you know how heavy those are? How much time and effort it'd take to move them overnight without me knowing? Yet still, that made more sense than them moving on their own, didn't it?"

He adjusted his shirt absently, scratching his arm.

"So, after that, I outfitted the park with security cameras and kept a closer eye on things. I hadn't made any sort of connection to the thunderstorm at that point, and it was a while before there was another one. But, sure enough, a late fall storm rolled through, and the damned things went wild."

Laughing, he added, "Being a recluse has a way of affecting your brain, but when I watched the camera monitors and saw my dinos stomping around and chasing each other, I thought I'd officially snapped. Eventually, I figured out I hadn't. That the impossible was actually happening."

"It makes zero sense," Laura said, staring at the man, but really looking through him. "This can't be possible. Did someone drug me and send me on the gnarliest trip of a lifetime? I—I just don't know that I can believe it. But..."

"But you do believe it."

She rubbed her face hard, if only to feel something rough, raw. "Fuck. Yeah, I guess I do believe it. Seeing is believing, right?"

The old man nodded.

"I'm still caught up on *how*, though," Laura said. "How how *how* does this happen? It doesn't *just happen*, that's the thing. Storms don't bring inanimate objects to life. It's lunacy. It's unreality."

"Eventually you come to accept it because, odd as it may seem, to not accept it is more dangerous. Physically, for sure, if you're foolhardy enough to go traipsing around while these beasts are running amok. But also, dangerous mentally. If you can't accept it, you run the risk of unmooring your base faculties. Who can you trust if you can't even trust your own eyes?"

"Deep," Laura said, unsure of how else to respond.

Again, Tippett seemed to not care about her reaction and continued. "*But*, I have a half-baked theory. I think it might have something to do with how they're constructed."

"What does that mean? How *are* they constructed?"

Tippett grinned. "There's real dinosaur bones in each and every one of them. A full damn skeleton of each species put together and held in place by a sculpted, resin body."

"Jesus. How did you even get all the bones? Wait, did you steal them? Never mind, I don't care. But wouldn't you, like, want to display the bones, seeing as how you are—were—a paleontologist?"

"My partner said something to that effect when I told him my plan to abandon the research world and open a theme park on the land I inherited. I had reservations at the time, sure, but I thought, what better way to utilize the bones than to use them in recreating the very animals they came from? And besides, if I ever wanted them back I knew how. I pulled the damned things from rock in the first place."

"Fair enough," she said, then they both went quiet for a minute. The rain had lessened significantly since sheltering in the terrarium building, and now she could barely hear it plinking against the terracotta shingles.

"You said *was* earlier, about your partner… What happened to them?"

The old man's face turned to a scowl before slowly softening again. "You really don't know what happened?"

Laura shook her head. "I'm not from around here. I know nothing about this place."

He nodded. "My partner, Phil…he's the reason I shut this place down. An…incident, here at the park… Well, he died."

"I'm sorry," she said, and meant it. Despite everything that had transpired in the past few hours. She knew what loss felt like. "Can I ask what the incident was?"

"Sure, it was a long time ago, after all. It was a freak accident. He was working on the trolley tracks, something simple, but it took longer than expected. The trolley tour guide didn't get the memo and brought a group out, then was too busy talking with the tour group and didn't see Phil still on the tracks. I guess people saw him struggling to get clear—his foot got caught, apparently—but no one bothered to say anything until it was too late."

"Oh my god. I'm…I'm so sorry," she said. "I am. But—But how you handled the loss, the grief, how was that the right thing to do? You shut down the park—fine. You hide out on your property, hide away from the world and everyone in it. Okay, no longer super great, but I guess a little understandable. I like my alone time, too. But then the whole dinosaurs coming to life thing happened and, like, you didn't bother to tell anyone? No warn—"

"And get tossed in a holding cell until deemed crazy? Miss, I don't think you understand rural Michigan. There's a reason my partner and I were only publicly *business partners* back then."

"I understand that, I do. *But*, you didn't *do* anything about the monsters— No, that's not right. You let them hunt. You have people *hunted* here. *Innocent* people. For Christ's sake." Her voice broke at the end, and she was breathing heavily.

"It's my private property. No one had to trespass," Tippett said with a shrug.

Her breath caught, Laura charged on. "Then, today. Forget warnings. Forget ignorance or abstention. You *tried* to get us all killed and you watched these people die and *you did nothing*. I mean, *fuck*, you're a goddamn sociopath, and I'm sitting here chatting you up like it's the end of the world and we're the last people in it."

Tippett held his lazy gaze on her face, his brown eyes simultaneously fierce and bored.

"Look," he said. "I don't need you to play pop psychologist with me. I don't have much concern about my moral ledger. I don't believe in a higher power or an afterlife. When I die—which, my dear, is likely to be soon—I'm dead. That's it. There's no more, and there's no judgment awaiting me. So please, save the rest of your breath."

Laura waved him off, as much dismissing him as herself. Not only was she too exhausted to argue, how did you argue with somehow who simply didn't care? A man who's been living in seclusion for years with nothing but randomly animated dinosaur statues. A certifiable—

A thought occurred to Laura just then. A nasty thought that made her feel nauseous. "Oh, no. Oh, Jesus Christ."

"What?"

"If the storms bring the dinosaurs to life, then when the storm is over they're back to statues. Isn't that right?"

"Indeed."

"So we could have just holed up in the gift shop and waited out the storm," she whispered. *Joel must have come to the park on a stormy night*, she thought. *Any other weather and he'd have been fine...*

"That's right. If you'd stayed hidden for a couple hours, the other two would still be alive."

"You bastard," she hissed, but the venom behind it was weak. She wanted to be mad—hell, *furious*. But she was so exhausted. The realization wiped out the meager reserves she had left after all the running and panic and tussling with that stupid little fucking monster outside. She had no time before to consider when she'd last eaten, but suddenly all she wanted was food. Her stomach ached and what she craved, for some reason, was a plate of loaded nachos.

The old man nodded once. No denial there.

Minutes of silence passed. When Tippett spoke, he startled her out of a half-asleep daze. "Okay, now I have a question for you."

Laura shrugged. *Whatever, just killing time, right?* she thought. Aloud: "Fine."

"You never told me why you're here. I'm curious why the others were here, but ultimately it doesn't much matter anymore. They're dead, and I will be sometime soon, I'm guessing. But you're here now, alive. So why? What brought you to my park of prehistoric horrors?"

This was it. She'd managed to avoid the topic during the entire conversation, despite this being the very reason she wanted to get to Tippett, and now it was time. She started to speak, then had to swallow away the excess saliva. "My brother—Joel. Joel Harding. He went missing a few weeks ago. I…I flew in from across the country to find him and found out he came here. This was the last place he was—"

The words caught in her throat, dwindling into a soft clicking noise. Tears sprang free and dribbled down her cheeks. Laura buried her head in her arm. She cried softly for a minute. Tippett stayed quiet, not consoling her, but not pushing her to continue talking, either.

When the tears subsided and she had better control over herself, she lifted her head. She intended to speak, but something pinged in her mind. Not a noise, but the absence of it. All was quiet, except if she strained her ears, the slight whooshing of a low breeze.

The rain. It had stopped. *The rain has stopped.*

The nightmare was over.

Laura leaped to her feet and went to the door. She wrenched it open, only barely registering the old man's pleas to *wait,* before stepping outside.

SEVENTEEN

Oh goddamnit, why didn't she listen to me? Was I not clear? Tippett thought as Laura slipped out into the unprotected and ruthless woods. He jumped to his feet, a motion that was more difficult and took longer than he wanted, though he *had* fallen out of the fucking treehouse.

He sidled through the half-open door, calling after Laura once again to wait, but with his voice low and full of concern. It was clear she didn't hear him. She'd run out into a small clearing, her arms raised and fool head scream-ing. Ironically, it was the very thing Tippett used to do as a kid, only he did so *in* the rain, not after it ended.

Feeling carefree and alive. He understood it, but he also understood how stupid she was being right now. But then, why did it matter? Why did he even care? He wanted her dead not even an hour ago. Had he grown an attach-ment to the young woman that quickly? And, how? Was it just because she was the first person to really talk to him in all these years? Maybe, maybe…

Tippett marched after her, reminding himself he hadn't heard anything in some time, so maybe they would be fine after—

He didn't hear it so much as feel it. The thunderous steps of one of his top predators. Maybe Rex, probably Spine. Laura didn't notice. She was too busy unleashing her demons.

When she finally stopped and dropped her arms, he was a few feet away. She smiled at him then, the most charming smile he'd seen since his partner had been ruthlessly taken from him. Toothy, full, and wide.

The comparison to the wide-open jaws of the Spinosaurus appearing behind her was so eerily similar as to be comical. But Tippett didn't laugh.

He said, "Not rain. *Electricity*. Run!" and saw, in the split second that followed, the dawning realization and terror-stricken expression flash on Laura's face.

Laura spun to face the towering dinosaur mid-attack just as Tippett reached her. He hooked his arm around her shoulder and threw her aside with as much force as he could muster.

His momentum carried him, half-bent, into the long, snapping jaws of the dinosaur. With the weight of boulders and the piercing of jagged glass, the Spinosaurus crunched down on his body.

Bones shattered. Organs popped. Flesh impaled, violated.

Tippett would have screamed if there had been any air in his lungs after the crushing impact.

Distantly, he heard Laura scream as Spine lifted him high into the air. Except—

Several seconds passed before Tippett realized he'd imagined being lifted. The dinosaur's movement had halted after only a couple feet. The dinosaur had frozen.

The storm had officially passed, and the dinosaur was, once again, a statue.

Tippett remained crushed in the immobile jaws, his limbs akimbo. The pain increased so fast it became white hot, then blipped out. As far as he was concerned, it was an act of mercy. Laura's shrieking wails warbled and rattled in his head, but over that noise he heard the steady flow and drip of liquid hitting the ground.

His blood. And by the sounds of it, he was losing it fast.

Didn't I always know it would end this way? he thought, somewhat deliriously. *Well, maybe not* this *way. But with the dinos. How did it go again? God created dinos, then killed them, then created man. Man killed God, created dinos, and then was killed by the dinos.*

It was the closest to a natural cycle that he could believe in.

Live, create, and die from the creation.

EIGHTEEN

"Laura, I'm—" he coughed, and more blood bubbled over his teeth and down his cheek. "I'm sorry."

"Hey, no, don't speak. Just…don't talk. Hang in there. I'll…" she trailed off. *I'll what, exactly?*

Tippett laughed pathetically. "Get help? No chance. I'll be dead in a minute. And—" another cough, "—you don't really want to save me, anyway. I'm—I'm not worth saving."

Laura grabbed his hand before she knew what she was doing. She squeezed it once, then let it go, unsure if either of them actually wanted the comforting.

"I'm sorry…about…Joel. I should have—" Violent coughs and spraying blood interrupted him. "Should've done something to help. I'm sorry."

The old man's face pulled in spots at the corners, a weak attempt at a conciliatory smile.

Laura offered one back.

"It's—" she started. There was no point going on. The man was dead.

Was she really going to say that it was okay? That she…what, forgave him? Or would it only have been an appeasement for a dying man? In that moment, she didn't have an answer. But she didn't need one, either. Alan Tippett was no longer listening.

Nobody was listening.

Gone. Each and every one of them. She didn't know most of them a few hours ago, and none of them a few weeks ago. Yet, their collective deaths weighed heavily on her already bruised soul. Realizing she'd never see Joel again was bad enough. But now, how could she process all of this? Could she ever even tell anyone what happened? She thought not. Not if she wanted to stay out of jail or close observation from a psychologist. Underneath it all, Laura caught a glimpse of pain and regret and…

Guilt.

But why? These weren't people she knew or even cared about, not in the grand scheme of things. They were all grown adults that got caught in the same shitstorm she had. Except—

Except how much of the decisions made were because of me?

The sheriff followed her in, so in that case, she was directly responsible for his being inside Prehistoric Park. Although, she had few fucks to give in his regard, callous as that may have seemed. Carly helped her look for clues which led them to the gate and helped usher in the events that brought them to the gift shop and beyond. Of course, Sam wanted to pursue Tippett as much as she did, but maybe if she had refused as steadfastly as Carly had tried to, things might have played out differently. Then there was Tippett, who sacrificed himself for her…

But I saved his ass first, she thought. *And he was trying to get us killed, remember?* Her internal monologue was harsh and angry, and for the moment, it worked. She snapped from her grief- and guilt-ridden reverie. The truth, she knew, was that not everything was her fault. Probably most, depending on the spin. In any case, she'd have a lifetime to ponder and worry and lose sleep over it. A lifetime she didn't think she'd see, only a short while ago.

She was the survivor. And what better way to honor those lost in the storm than to live?

After checking the time, she figured she had only an hour or so of light left. So, despite the lack of urgency in terms of dangerous dinosaurs, she still had to hurry and find a way out. Spending the night in this land of death and mayhem was not an option.

She repositioned herself on the path and got her bearings. Facing more or less due north, she began her march through the woods. Eventually—and hopefully soon—she'd hit the fence. She'd find a way over, just like she had when she arrived. After that, drive to the nearest airport without stopping. No police, no parents, no*body*.

The only thing Laura intended to do now was fly the fuck home and never set foot in Michigan again.

ACKNOWLEDGMENTS

Books don't happen without help, and this one is no exception. Let's share some thanks.

First and foremost, this book does not exist without *Jurassic Park*. Crichton, Spielberg, and Williams. I'm not the same person if their art never entered my life.

I'm forever thankful for my family. The constant love and support as I continue this endeavor is really all I need. To my little dude, thanks for all your excitement about this book (even if it's only because the dinosaur art is so cool). Special thanks to Korie and my parents for being willing to take early looks at my stories when I ask.

Big thanks to Alexis, as always, for being such a great beta-buddy on this book (like all the other times).

To Alex Woodroe, for your brilliant editing eye, invaluable publishing advice, and friendship.

With regards to the book and its appearance, a massive thanks to Camila Alli Chair Montá for gracing the cover with the absolute perfect art and stunning interior illustrations.

Some final thanks are owed to you, dear reader. I tend to get a little sick of my books by the time they're ready for publication. But that's okay, it's in your hands now. The fact that you're here means the world to me.

ABOUT THE AUTHOR

Alex Ebenstein is a lifelong Michigander, where he lives with his wife, son, and dog. His daytime mapmaking career supports his nighttime addiction of writing horror and other speculative fiction. His debut horror novella, *Curse Corvus*, was released in April 2023, and his follow-up novella, *Melon Head Mayhem*, was released by Shortwave Publishing in July 2023. He is also the editor of the SPLIT SCREAM series, published by Tenebrous Press. Connect with him on social media @AlexEbenstein and keep up with writing news at alexebenstein.com.

CONTENT WARNINGS

Reanimated Rex contains scenes that deal with:
*Death of/harm to a child
*Graphic or explicit death on page
*Sexism and misogyny

Please be advised.

SPRUCE ROAD

SAUROPOD SWAMP

BRACHIOSAURUS

SPINOSAURUS

JURASSIC JUNGLE

TERTIARY TERRARIUM

TYRANNOSAURUS REX

TRIASSIC TREEHOUSE

PACHYCEPH-ALOSAURUS

TRICERATOPS

DINO DEPOT

UTAHRAPTOR

PROCOMP-SOGNATHUS

CRETACEOUS CAFÉ

FOSSIL DIG

STEGOSAURUS

PARASAUR-OLOPHUS

GIFT SHOP

ALLOSAURUS

ANKYLOSAURUS

P

FRONTIER ROAD

PREHISTORIC PARK

Ankles

Stego

Pachy

Utes

Tricera

Allo

READ MORE FROM
ALEX EBENSTEIN

A flock of birds fallen from the sky. A wedding dress billowing with the specter of its deserter...

The fevered pursuit of happiness comes at a cost, and toxic positivity has never been more lethal.

"An unforgettable and perfectly chilling portent."
-Lauren Bolger, author of *Kill Radio*

"Expertly captures the dizzying flight of devoted friendship beset by an insidious supernatural threat."
-Gordon B. White, Shirley Jackson Award and Bram Stoker Award Finalist

alexebenstein.com

It's a creature feature. It's a throwback. It's…
MELON HEAD MAYHEM!

"The modern day Goosebumps for adults."
-*Horror Obsessive*

"Pure creature feature goodness"
-Joshua Hull, author of *Mouth* and screenwriter of *Glorious*

"A fast-paced and fun love letter to the days of VHS tapes"
-Angela Sylvaine, author of *Frost Bite*

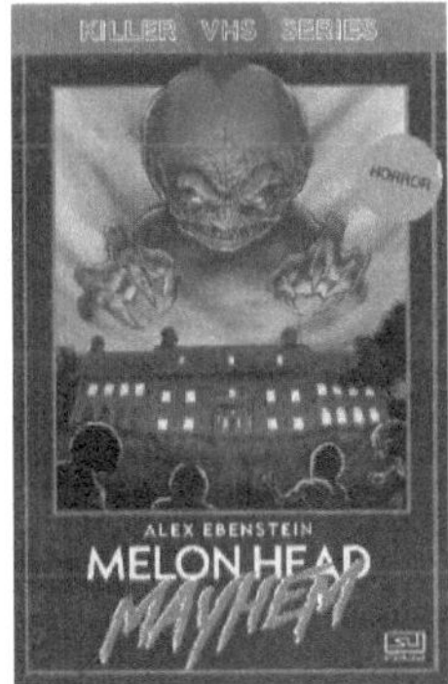

shortwavepublishing.com

9 781960 470034